"As a matter of fact," Chris went on, suddenly sounding a bit mischievous, "I just thought of a code name for our undercover investigation of Mr. Stone and the workings of the Ridgewood Children's Hospital. Something that's right in line with Christmas. . . ."

Susan couldn't resist. "All right. What's the code name you thought up?" she asked with a grin.

"The Candy Cane Caper! It's perfect, don't you think?"

"It *is* kind of catchy," Susan had to agree. She thought for a minute, then said, "Well, Chris, you can certainly be persuasive. It's true that, at this point, we don't have very much to go on. Nothing more than a rumor, really. But if there's even the slightest chance that you and I could find out what's going on and keep the children's hospital from having to close . . . well, how could I possibly say no to that?"

Fawcett Juniper Books
by Cynthia Blair:

THE BANANA SPLIT AFFAIR

THE CANDY CANE CAPER

FREEDOM TO DREAM

THE HOT FUDGE SUNDAY AFFAIR

MARSHMALLOW MASQUERADE

THE PUMPKIN PRINCIPLE

STARSTRUCK

STRAWBERRY SUMMER

THE
CANDY CANE
CAPER

Cynthia Blair

FAWCETT JUNIPER   •   NEW YORK

RLI: $\dfrac{\text{VL: 5 + up}}{\text{IL: 6 + up}}$

A Fawcett Juniper Book
Published by Ballantine Books
Copyright © 1987 by Cynthia Blair

Library of Congress Catalog Card Number: 87-91538

ISBN 0-449-70221-9

All the characters in this book are fictitious, and any resemblance to persons living or dead is purely coincidental.

Manufactured in the United States of America

First Edition: December 1987

One

"Christine Pratt, what on earth *are you doing?"*

Susan Pratt had just strolled into her twin sister's bedroom, planning to show her the Christmas card that had arrived in the mail earlier that morning, the very first one of the holiday season. She expected to find her twin whiling away this cold Saturday morning in early December listening to music or daydreaming or perhaps even doing some homework. Instead, the seventeen-year-old girl had opened the bedroom window up wide and was leaning out as far as she possibly could.

Despite her sister's alarm, however, Chris was quite matter-of-fact.

"I was looking for snow," she replied with a discouraged sigh. She turned around to face her twin, slamming the window shut behind her. "And I couldn't be more disappointed. Between the bright sun and that blue sky—not to mention those puffy white clouds up there—I don't think a single snowflake is on its way!"

Wearing a deep frown, Chris plopped down on her bed. "At this rate, not only will the Pratts of Whittington not see a white Christmas this year; I'll never be able to muster up a *drop* of holiday spirit!"

Susan couldn't help laughing at her twin's distress. "Don't despair, Chris. I suspect that holiday spirit is contagious—and that means you should be catching it from me any minute now! And believe me: I've got a very serious case of yuletide fever!"

It was true; as far as Susan Pratt was concerned, this brisk wintry day was the perfect time to welcome in the holiday season, and she had already gotten the festivities under way. That morning she had whipped up a tremendous batch of gingerbread dough and cut it into different shapes with cookie cutters, stars and bells and wreaths and even gingerbread boys and girls. In fact, at that very moment, her second trayful of cookies was baking in the oven.

"Besides," Susan went on, "as soon as I show you what we just got in the mail this morning, I bet you'll change your mind."

"Oooh, what is it?" Chris squealed, rushing over to see what her sister was hiding behind her back. "A present? A fruitcake? Or maybe an invitation to a Christmas party?"

"Sorry to disappoint you. It's only a Christmas card—but it's the very first one this year." Susan handed it over to her sister. "And it *is* kind of pretty. . . ."

"A Christmas card? Well, I suppose that *is* one sure sign that Christmas is just around the corner. Even so, I'm still not feeling any Christmas spirit. . . ."

"At least take a look at the card!" Susan pretended to be exasperated.

Chris took the card out of its envelope and studied the picturesque snow scene on the front. A quiet New England town complete with farms and houses, old-fashioned horse-drawn sleighs, and a quaint white church with a steeple was covered in snow. The snow practically glowed in the soft yellow moonlight. It was a lovely card, and Chris really did feel moved—as if something deep inside her were starting to realize that Christmas was, indeed, less than three weeks away.

"It *is* pretty, Sooz," Chris admitted. "And that looks like the perfect place to celebrate the holidays, doesn't it? I can just imagine going for a sleigh ride on a cold, snowy night and then coming home to a warm house with a fire burning in the fireplace and a huge Christmas tree, all decorated . . ."

"Stop!" Susan cried. "You're making me wish it were Christmas right *now*! At the rate I'm going, I'll *never* be able to wait until December twenty-fifth!"

"You've forgotten one thing." Chris was suddenly serious as she sank down onto the bed once again. Pensively she began to pet Jonathan, the girls' cat, who had just wandered into the room, leaped up on the bed beside her, and purred insistently, demanding attention. "We're not going to have much of a Christmas if we don't get some snow soon. Oh, I wish we lived in the town in the picture!"

Susan looked at the card once more. "You know, Chris, this town reminds me of a real place. Someplace we've both been. Someplace where there's lots and lots of snow in the winter. . . ."

"Ridgewood!" Chris exclaimed. "Of course! It *does* look like Ridgewood!"

The town that Chris and Susan were thinking of was a small town in Vermont where their grandparents lived. Although their father's parents, John and Emily Pratt, came to Whittington every year to spend the Christmas holidays with their son and his family, the girls hadn't been up to their house in years. Even so, they had only the fondest memories of the quaint New England village nestled in among the snow-covered hills and fragrant pine forests.

Even though Ridgewood was close to several of the popular ski resorts in the area, it had managed to remain untouched by crowds of tourists. It consisted of just a few stores and public buildings surrounded by a scattering of houses that looked very much like those in the picture.

"Gee, Sooz, I just had a wonderful idea," Chris suddenly said. "What if we all went up to New England and spent Christmas up there this year, instead of having Grandma and Grandpa come here? We'd have plenty of snow, and fires in the fireplace, and sleigh rides. . . ."

"It sounds too good to be true." Susan thought for a minute, then frowned. "But there's one problem with that plan."

"Really? What?"

"Well, we've always had Christmas here in this house ever since we were born. It's become kind of a family tradition. And, frankly, I have a feeling that Mom and Dad would be disappointed if we wanted to go someplace else for the holidays."

"I know what you mean," Chris agreed. She was pensive for a few seconds . . . and then her face lit up. "Hey, I have an idea! Maybe you and I could come up with some kind of prank that would allow us to celebrate Christmas in Ridgewood without disappointing Mom and Dad!"

Susan smiled mischievously. "Maybe we could. After all, we've certainly managed to pull off some terrific capers in the past!"

That was no exaggeration; Susan and Chris already had quite a history of playing practical jokes. And more often than not, they took advantage of the fact that they were identical twins in order to do something that they wouldn't have been able to do otherwise—sometimes to help other people out, sometimes just to have fun, but almost always learning some important lessons along the way.

And they did, indeed, look similar. Both girls had the same chestnut-brown hair, now cut short as the result of their most recent adventure, the *Marshmallow Masquerade*, in which Chris pretended to be a teenaged boy for a week so the twins could learn something about what made the opposite sex tick. They also had identical features: dark brown eyes, perky ski-jump noses, and high cheekbones.

Despite their similar appearances, however, Susan and Chris were really very different. Susan was quiet and shy, and her favorite hobbies were reading and painting. In fact, she hoped to go to art school after high school graduation. Chris, on the other hand, was outgoing and talkative, preferring to spend her free time going out with friends or talking on the phone. She was a member of both Whittington High's girls' swimming team and the cheerleading squad, and she often participated in afterschool activities like the Dance Committee.

Both girls, however, had a few things in common. They were both bright, quick-thinking, fun-loving . . . and they would go to almost any lengths in order to carry out one of their mischievous pranks.

At the moment, however, none of these traits seemed to be serving them very well. Although they had both lapsed into silence, daydreaming about how spending Christmas in a quaint Vermont village would be like something out of a fairy tale, at the moment neither one of them could come up with a single idea as to how to make that fairy tale come true.

"Oh, well," Chris suddenly said with a sigh. "I guess you and I will end up spending Christmas in good old Whittington again. I, for one, can't think of any way we could talk Mom and Dad into spending the holidays away from home."

"Well, it's not so bad." Susan tried to sound optimistic.

"Maybe it's not the most exciting or adventurous or *romantic* place in the world, but you and I have always managed to have a merry Christmas before!"

Suddenly she snapped out of her dreamy state. "Hey, look at the time! It's eleven-thirty, time for me to take my second batch of gingerbread cookies out of the oven! Want to help?"

"Sure." Lazily Chris dragged herself off the bed. "Maybe the smell of fresh gingerbread will help put me in a holiday mood."

"Or maybe washing bowls and wooden spoons and cookie sheets will!" Her sister laughed. "I sure hope so. I could use a hand!"

When the twins scrambled into the kitchen, whooping and laughing as they teased each other about who had done more baking over the years—and who had done the majority of the cleaning up—they found their parents sitting at the table, munching gingerbread boys and girls with raisin eyes, noses, and mouths from Susan's first batch of cookies.

"Whoa—you caught us red-handed!" chortled Mr. Pratt, guiltily clapping his hand over his mouth. "Don't blame me, I couldn't resist! Surely you couldn't expect me to be in the same room as freshly baked cookies and not eat at least *one*!"

"One!" Mrs. Pratt exclaimed. "Why, if I'm not mistaken, I'd say I've already seen you devour at least five of these poor little gingerbread people!"

"Five! Not five!" Mr. Pratt protested. "Well . . . maybe. But I was just *testing* them for you. You should *thank* me!"

"It's okay, Daddy." Susan laughed as she picked up two potholders, took her second tray out of the oven, and slid in a third. "That's what cookies are for—to eat. Especially Christmas cookies!"

"I don't know about that," Chris teased. "I think that there should be some kind of law that says no one is allowed to eat a single Christmas cookie until there are at least three inches of snow on the ground."

"In that case"—Susan groaned—"we might *never* get to eat any!"

The twins noticed then that their parents were suddenly looking very serious. It had all started when Chris first mentioned snow. . . .

"It's funny you should say that," said their father. "We were just talking about that very subject. Snow, I mean."

"That's right," Mrs. Pratt agreed. "We were both saying how nice it would be to get away from all this cold weather for a change."

Susan and Chris exchanged worried glances.

"As a matter of fact," Mrs. Pratt went on, "we were talking about how nice it would be to go someplace warm for Christmas. Someplace exotic. Someplace . . . well, someplace like Mexico."

"Mexico!" the girls cried in unison.

"But there's *never* any snow in Mexico!" Chris wailed.

Mr. Pratt cleared his throat. "Your mother and I were thinking that maybe the two of us would go together . . . alone. You know, as sort of a second honeymoon."

"That sounds like a great idea," Susan said heartily. "But . . . what about us?"

"Well, we were thinking that you girls might like to visit your grandparents for the holidays, instead of having them come here." Mrs. Pratt looked from one of her daughters to the other, a hopeful look on her face. "I know we wouldn't all be together, but you'd still get to see Grandma and Grandpa. . . ."

"And there'd be plenty of snow," Mr. Pratt interjected. "December in Vermont practically guarantees that!"

"And I just know they'd love to have you spend your school vacation with them. Why, it's been years since you've been up to New England. They're always asking us when their two favorite grandchildren are going to come for a visit." Nervously Mrs. Pratt asked, "So, girls, what do you think?"

Chris and Susan looked at each other . . . and then burst out laughing.

"It looks as if we'll be enjoying a white Christmas after all!" Susan cried.

"I'll say it does!" Chris agreed. "And do you know what, Sooz? Maybe it's the smell of gingerbread, maybe it's the prospect of spending Christmas in Vermont . . . but all of a sudden, I'm positively *bursting* with yuletide cheer!"

"Terrific!" Susan exclaimed. "Why don't we go call Grandma and Grandpa right away and tell them that their 'two favorite grandchildren' are going to be arriving soon . . . ?"

"And that they'd better brace themselves," Chris added merrily. "Because the two of us are going to be bringing along so much Christmas spirit that a town the size of Ridgewood will never forget it!"

As Chris happily popped a gingerbread star into her mouth, she never suspected how true her teasing prediction would turn out to be.

Two

"*Do you see what I see, Sooz?*"

Chris had just woken up from a catnap, but her eyes, still heavy with sleep, suddenly grew round as she looked out the window of the bus. "*Snow!* Look at it! There's snow *everywhere!*"

Susan, who had been awake during the entire bus ride out of Montpelier, wasn't at all surprised by the winter wonderland that surrounded them as they sped down the highway toward Ridgewood. After all, she had been staring out the window, enthralled, the whole time. And she had been enjoying every minute, even though so far there was little to see besides the snow-covered pine forests that lined both sides of the road. Just knowing that she was in Vermont was enough to get her so caught up in making plans that she felt as if at any minute she might jump out of her seat, rush to the front of the bus, and beg the driver to get them to their destination even faster.

"You're right, Chris! That white stuff all over the place has simply *got* to be snow!" Teasingly, Susan added, "How's your Christmas spirit *now?*"

"Well," Chris returned, her brown eyes twinkling merrily, "let's just say that if we could somehow manage to harness all my Christmas spirit, we could easily run this bus with it!"

It was Saturday afternoon, exactly two weeks after the twins and their parents had decided that the girls would spend their school vacation in Vermont while Mr. and Mrs. Pratt flew off to warm, sunny Mexico for their holiday. It was also one week before Christmas. Early that morning, Chris and Susan had flown into Montpelier, then hopped onto a bus headed for the small town in which their grandparents lived. With each passing mile, Susan grew more and more excited, even though her twin took advantage of the end of their journey to rest up before descending upon Ridgewood—and officially beginning her Christmas vacation in a place that looked as if it were Santa Claus's real headquarters.

When the bus stopped in Ridgewood a few mintues later, it took Chris and Susan only a few seconds to gather up the things they had brought along with them for their weeklong stay at their grandparents': two small suitcases, two pairs of ice skates, one pair of skis, two shopping bags filled with presents from their parents, and a huge tin stuffed to the limit with an assortment of the Christmas cookies that Susan had been baking ever since she and her twin found out that their dream of spending the holidays in a snow-covered New England village was going to come ture.

Juggling all their belongings was no small feat. Fortunately, it wasn't long before they got some assistance.

"Hey, there, need some help?" asked a friendly but unfamiliar voice.

Chris turned and found herself face-to-face with a boy who looked as if he were about her age, with red hair, green eyes, and an impish grin.

"Do . . . do I know you?" she asked, a bit confused.

"No, you don't, as a matter of fact," the boy said. "But I think I know you. Or at least who you are. That is, if I'm not seeing double. . . ."

"You're not," Susan assured him with a chuckle. "There really *are* two of us."

"In that case, I guess it's a pretty safe bet that you're Susan and Christine Pratt, right? Well, I'm Andy Connors. I do odd jobs for your grandfather after school and on weekends. I offered to come pick you girls up this afternoon to save him a trip." He looked over at all the suitcases, shopping bags, and sports equipment that the girls were struggling with. "How long are you girls planning to stay, anyway?"

Chris and Susan burst out laughing.

"Let's just say that we believe in being prepared for anything," Susan quipped.

"That's right," Chris agreed. "When it comes to having a good time, Sooz and I don't leave a single thing up to chance!"

"By the way, I'm Chris, and this is my sister, Susan."

"Hi, Chris. Hi, Susan. Listen, I have a question: Is there any convenient way of telling you two apart?"

"It's easy once you get to know us," Susan insisted. "We may look the same, but we're really very different."

Andy looked skeptical. "If you say so. . . . Anyway, I'll figure all that out later. In the meantime let's get this stuff into the trunk of my car and get on our way. I know for a fact that there are two people waiting for you . . . and they're very anxious to see you!"

Sure enough, as Andy's car pulled up in front of John and Emily Pratt's home, a white shingled Colonial-style house with a big front porch, a white picket fence, and a smiling snowman in the front yard, both Mr. and Mrs. Pratt were standing in the doorway eagerly watching the road as they waited for their two granddaughters to show up.

"Grandma! Grandpa!" the twins cried as they scrambled out of the car and raced up the walk. "It's so great to see you!"

It was, indeed, wonderful to see them again: John Pratt, with his thick gray hair, gentle manner, and sense of humor—something he had passed on to his son, the girls' father; and Emily Pratt, equally warm and generous, always going out of her way to make her "two favorite grand-daughters" feel welcome.

"How was your trip up here?" asked Mr. Pratt, once all four had exchanged hugs and kisses and the twins had passed on their parents' regards.

"It was a breeze," said Chris.

"How would *you* know?" her twin teased. "After all, you slept through at least half of it!"

"Well, at any rate, you two must be famished," said Mrs. Pratt. "Come on into the dining room and have some hot chocolate. I also baked some of your favorite goodies. . . ."

Laughing, Susan held up the tin of cookies she had brought along. "Well, one thing's for sure: Even if we get snowed in over the holidays, we don't have to worry about there being a shortage of Christmas cookies!"

The girls took a quick tour of the first floor of the house while Andy brought their suitcases upstairs to their rooms. Their grandparents had instituted quite a few changes since their last visit almost three years before. There was new apple-green flowered wallpaper in the living room, a friendly room with comfortable chairs and a big soft couch. And there was now a colorful rag rug in the middle of the room, one that the handy Mrs. Pratt had made herself. There were other, smaller changes as well: some new lamps, a fresh coat of paint on the walls, an updated family photograph of the twins and their parents, hung right next to the wooden stairway so that any visitor to the house was sure to see it.

Some things were still the same, however—like the huge stone fireplace that lined one entire wall of the living room. There was a huge fire burning in it this afternoon, but that was not the only welcoming touch. There was also a huge Christmas tree scenting the entire room with a strong pine fragrance that was guaranteed to put even Ebenezer Scrooge into a holiday mood. Pine garlands dotted with candy canes were looped over the mantelpiece, and fresh pine wreaths were hung in every window on the entire first floor.

"It looks as if Christmas is already well under way here!" Susan commented as she and her sister continued with their tour by wandering into the dining room.

That was also an inviting room. In it was a long dining room table covered with a beautiful tablecloth, a patchwork of red and green Christmas fabrics, handmade by Emily Pratt. There were also red candles in the middle of the table along with a big bowl of Christmas candy.

"I'll say it has!" Chris agreed. "If you and I wanted to have a real old-fashioned Christmas celebration this year, we definitely came to the right place!"

The twins sat down at the table with their grandparents, anxious to chat with them. The four of them had so much to catch up on! The letters and telephone calls of the past year suddenly seemed as if they had been so inadequate . . . and Chris and Susan wanted to tell them about a million different things at once. They chattered away about school and their friends and even all the pranks they had been playing lately, all the while enjoying hot chocolate and at least six different varieties of Christmas cookies, all of them of course homemade.

Finally, when all four Pratts were convinced that eating even one more mouthful would simply be impossible, Susan said, "You know, Chris, you and I have been talking away for the past hour a mile a minute. We've barely given Grandma and Grandpa a chance to say a word!"

She turned to them and said, "Now we promise to be quiet for a while so you can tell us everything that *you've* been doing!"

Suddenly John and Emily Pratt grew serious. They looked at each other as if they were trying to decide whether or not this was the best time to say what was really on their minds. Chris and Susan noticed their hesitancy immediately—and quickly grew concerned.

"Is . . . is everything all right?" asked Susan. "You both look so worried all of a sudden."

"Well, we're not really *worried* . . ." said Mrs. Pratt. "I suppose we're just a little afraid of how you girls will take the news we've got to tell you."

"What news?" the twins asked in unison.

"Oh, it's not such a terrible thing!" Mr. Pratt insisted in a hearty voice. "Your grandmother and I have simply decided that it's time for us to move to a warmer climate, that's all. Buy ourselves a condominium down in Florida, in one of those retirement villages. Start taking things a little bit easier."

"Move?" Chris blinked. "You two are going to move?"

"But what about the house?" Susan asked.

"We'll have to sell it," Mrs. Pratt said softly. "Certainly we feel bad about that. . . ."

"Sell your house!" Chris squealed. "You can't do that! Why, you two have lived up here in this house ever since . . . well, even before Dad was born!"

"Besides, you can't move to a retirement village!" Susan insisted. "You're too young!"

Mr. and Mrs. Pratt chuckled.

"I'm afraid we're anything but young," said Mr. Pratt. No, Emily and I have decided that it's just time, that's all."

"But you're still young at heart," Susan insisted.

"Oh, pooh," scoffed Emily Pratt. "John and I are getting so old that we're not much good for anything anymore. Your grandfather and I are just two old-timers."

"That's nonsense, Grandma and Grandpa!" Chris protested. "Besides, I thought you loved this town. You know practically everyone who lives here, you know every single tree and hill, you're both so busy with your lives here . . . why, the town of Ridgewood is *part* of you!"

"It's true, it will be a big adjustment." Emily Pratt sighed. "But your grandfather is right, it *is* time. And we'll manage to make new friends once we get down there.

"Besides, don't forget that owning a house is a lot of work. Things will be much simpler for us in a condominium. We'll have more time for the things we enjoy but just don't seem to be able to find the time for. Like my sewing. There are so many craft projects I've been longing to work on but just never get around to, what with all the work involved in keeping this place running. . . ."

"Have you told Mom and Dad about this yet?" Susan asked. Chris knew immediately what her sister was thinking; if *they* couldn't talk their grandparents out of this crazy idea of selling their house, the place they loved most in the whole world, maybe their parents could.

"No, we haven't," Mrs. Pratt said, shaking her head. "We decided to wait until after Christmas. We didn't want to upset them right before their second honeymoon. But we will as soon as they get back.

"Now enough about this! Why don't you two scoot up to your rooms and take a look around? We've made some changes up there, too. I've given you the two attic rooms, the ones with the sloping walls and all the alcoves. They were always your favorites when you were little girls. I've redecorated them both, and I'm anxious to see how you like them. . . ."

It was with heavy hearts that Susan and Chris trudged up the two flights of stairs, up to the two bedrooms that, indeed, had always been their favorite rooms at their grandparents' house. They brightened a bit when they saw them, however. Susan's had been covered with pale blue wallpaper sprigged with tiny white flowers—the exact same print as her favorite flannel nightgown, which she had brought along for snuggling under a fluffy down quilt during the cold Vermont nights. There was a blue-and-white-patchwork bedspread and a blue rag rug, both of them handmade by her grandmother. Chris's room was identical—except that the wallpaper and everything else was a pale yellow.

Chris plopped her suitcase down on the bed and half-heartedly began to unpack. Across the hallway, she could hear her sister doing the same thing—with just as much reluctance. It didn't take her long to abandon her project and stroll into her sister's bedroom.

"Suddenly all my Christmas spirit has gone out the window," she complained. "I can't believe that Grandma and Grandpa are planning to sell this place!"

"I know," Susan agreed, sitting down on the bed, her shoulders sagging. "They're too young to move to a retirement village. Too energetic. Besides, they *love* this place! It's their *home*!"

The girls were quiet for a minute.

And then Susan said, "You know, I wonder if there's anything we can do to change their minds."

"Do you really think we could, Sooz?"

"Well . . . I'm not sure, exactly. But we do have a few

things in our favor. For one, Grandma and Grandpa must be experiencing a few of their own doubts. Otherwise they wouldn't have waited until after Mom and Dad's vacation before telling them."

Chris brightened. "That's true! What did Grandma say? That she didn't want to upset them? That means they might realize, deep in their hearts, that maybe it's not such a good idea after all."

"Right. And here's something else in our favor. We're *here*. We have a whole week, from now until Christmas, to change their minds."

"Of course! And there's one more thing. . . ."

Susan looked puzzled. "What's that, Chris?"

"You and I happen to be experts when it comes to thinking up clever little schemes. Surely you and I can come up with *some* way of convincing Grandma and Grandpa that they're still young at heart!"

Susan nodded. "You've got a point there. If anyone can do it, Chris, we can." She thought for a minute. "As a matter of fact, we could start thinking of that as our goal for the next few days. Oh, sure, we've been planning on wrapping Christmas presents and singing carols and going for sleigh rides, but this is something that's really crucial. And I bet if we put our heads together, we could come up with something. . . ."

"I'll bet we could, too," Chris said. But she sounded anything but optimistic. At the moment she couldn't come up with a single idea. And suddenly it seemed as if it were really important that she and her sister do something. More important than their vacation, more important than having a good time . . . more important, even, than Christmas itself.

"Yes, I'm not at all worried," she said, trying to convince herself that that was true. "Maybe I can't think of anything right now, but I'll bet you anything that sooner or later one of us will!''

But as she wandered over to her bedroom window and looked out at the quaint snowy town of Ridgewood down below, she was wishing she could make a telephone call to Santa Claus. And she knew exactly what she would ask him for: a surefire way of convincing John and Emily Pratt that the best thing for them to do was forget all about this silly notion of selling their beloved house and moving to a condominium in a retirement village!

Three

By the next morning Chris and Susan had pushed aside all their dismay over their grandparents' announcement that they planned to sell their house and move south. They were too excited about their first full day in Vermont—and too busy making plans.

"Ooh, just *look* at all that gorgeous snow!" Chris cried, leaning out the open window in her bedroom as far as she could without falling. "If I don't get outside within the next thirty seconds, I'm going to *scream*!"

It was late Sunday morning, and she and her twin had just finished a huge breakfast in the pleasant dining room: a huge stack of light, fluffy pancakes topped with butter and, of course, hot Vermont maple syrup. But instead of feeling weighed down by all the food she'd just eaten, Chris was raring to go. In fact, she was getting ready to go ice-skating on the big pond right down the road, putting a down vest over the blue and white ski sweater she was already wearing with a pair of blue corduroy pants.

"Are you sure you're going to be warm enough?" Susan asked doubtfully. She was in her bedroom, right across the hall, getting dressed to go outside herself. She, however, was bundling up in two sweaters, a coat, a muffler, earmuffs, and the thickest wool mittens she had.

Chris turned to look at her twin—and then burst out laughing.

"Susan Pratt! You look like a snowman with all those clothes on!"

"Well . . . it's cold out there! After all, this is Vermont! And what about you? You're going to *freeze* out there!"

Chris shook her head. "Not me. Once I get out on that ice, whirling and twirling all over the place, I'll be as warm as toast." She picked up her ice skates and headed for the door. "Besides," she added with a twinkle in her brown eyes, "you seem to be forgetting that one of the best parts of ice-skating is drinking hot chocolate in front of a roaring fire right afterward!"

As she hurried down the stairs, more anxious than ever to feel the smooth ice speeding by underneath the blades of her skates and the brisk wind on her cheeks, Chris called over her shoulder, "Good luck with your Christmas shopping, Sooz! I bet you'll find the perfect gift for everyone on your list before you know it!"

Susan was much less optimistic than her sister. While she was looking forward to spending the afternoon browsing in Ridgewood's shops, she had yet to come up with any really good ideas for Christmas presents. And this year, especially, she wanted to get something special for Chris and her grandparents.

"Oh, well," she said aloud. "Maybe I'll get some ideas once I'm actually in those cute little shops."

She checked her appearance in the mirror over her dresser . . . and she couldn't help giggling. Chris was right, she *did* look like a snowman! Susan took off one of her two sweaters. She was about to leave her red woolen scarf behind as well but at the last minute decided to wear it, just in case it turned out to be windier than she expected.

The town of Ridgewood was very much the way she remembered it. There were only a few stores in the center in the town, lining the village green—which today was anything *but* green. As a matter of fact, it was covered in pure white snow, smooth and untouched and glistening in the bright December sun.

That is, all except for one corner, right near the church that sat at one edge of the green. There the snow had obviously been tromped through, rolled in—and used to build the biggest snowman that Susan had ever seen. It was almost finished, and it stood well over seven feet tall, she estimated. It had thick branches for arms, with the tiny branches at the very end forming fingers.

And its face was the friendliest snowman face she had ever seen. Its eyes, made of black squares of coal, seemed to twinkle in the sunlight, and its coal mouth turned upward in a huge mischievous grin. It had a carrot nose and a funny black hat, which the two people who were making this wonderful snow creation were putting on top of its head. A young man was holding a little boy, his building partner, on his shoulders. The boy was laughing loudly as he reached over and, with great ceremony, placed the hat on top of the snowman's head.

Susan wasn't in any real hurry, and she couldn't resist strolling over to the edge of the village green to get a better look at the snowman. As she got closer, she saw that the older boy looked as if he were about her age. The younger boy was probably about seven or eight. She noticed that he had a cast on one arm, as if it had been sprained or broken.

As soon as the two boys spotted her, they broke into proud grins that were almost as big as the snowman's.

"Hello, there!" called the older boy. "What do you think of our big snowy friend here?"

"He's fantastic!" Susan replied shyly. "Does he have a name?"

"Sure!" said the little boy, turning to his friend. "His name is Brian Barker—just like yours!"

Brian the human laughed. "Okay, Danny. If you want to call him Brian Barker, then Brian Barker it is!"

Susan could see that these two boys meant a great deal to each other. She wondered if they were brothers. Close up, however, they looked very different. Brian had blond hair and blue eyes, while Danny had dark brown hair and hazel eyes. Perhaps they were just friends. . . .

"You know, this snowman of yours really needs something," Susan said, cocking her head and examining it carefully.

Brian and Danny looked disappointed. "Really? What have we forgotten?"

Susan walked up to Brian the snowman, took off her red wool muffler, and tied it around his neck.

"There!" she said, standing back to study the effect. "Now he's perfect!"

Danny chortled gleefully. "Oh, thank you! You're right, that's exactly what he needed!" He paused, then turned to face her. "You're so nice, giving our snowman your scarf and all, and I don't even know who you are. Do you live in Ridgewood?"

"No, I'm just visiting. My name is Susan Pratt, and my grandparents, John and Emily Pratt, live here in town. My sister and I are spending the Christmas holidays with them this year."

"Gee, that sounds great," Danny said wistfully. "Being able to spend Christmas with your family, I mean."

What an odd thing to say! Susan thought. Aloud, she

said, "Maybe you'd like to come visit me there sometime this week and meet my family. I have a sister, and there's my grandparents, of course. And maybe you'd like to see the wonderful Christmas tree in the living room. . . ."

"Wow! Really? You really mean it?" Danny looked as if she had just promised him a visit to Santa Claus's home in the North Pole itself.

"I'm looking forward to it, Danny!"

"I hope that invitation is being extended to me as well," Brian said teasingly. "I always enjoy visiting people during the Christmas holidays."

"Well, then, you'll both have to come. We can have tea—and all the homemade Christmas cookies you can eat! Both my grandmother and I love to bake."

"Oh, boy!" cried Danny. "A Christmas tree, homemade cookies . . . This might turn out to be a real Christmas after all!"

Susan looked at him, even more surprised than before. She was on the verge of asking him why on earth this *wouldn't* be a real Christmas, then decided against it.

"I have some shopping to do right now," she said, "but I'll tell you what. You two can feel free to stop over any time you please. That address is Thirty-three Ridgewood Street. I'll be around."

"Okay!" said Danny, now wearing a grin that was easily even bigger than the snowman's. "Brian and I will see you soon!"

Susan was still feeling a bit puzzled as she strolled back to Ridgewood's string of stores. She was wondering if Brian and Danny were brothers or friends, how they came to know each other if they were just friends, how Danny had broken his arm . . . and, most of all, what he had meant when he made that peculiar comment about Christmas. But she quickly forgot all about the mysterious twosome as she began to browse in Ridgewood's intriguing shops.

She bypassed the stores that catered to the local residents: a small supermarket, a drugstore, a dry cleaners. Aside from those, however, there were some that were perfect for browsing, and since this was the week before Christmas, all of them were open. There was a bookstore, in which Susan found a brand-new book of photographs of the Vermont countryside that would be the perfect gift for her grandparents—especially since she hadn't forgotten her vow of the night before to work with her sister to help change their minds about moving away from the state they loved so much. There was a gourmet food shop, where she bought some maple candy molded into maple leaf shapes for Chris. She got an extra box to bring home to her parents, along with a small jug of real Vermont maple syrup.

Her favorite place, however, was a shop called Betty's that sold craft supplies. She wanted to get something for her grandmother, and she found some beautiful yarn, soft and fuzzy, a blend of different shades of purple and lavender. She decided to specify on the gift card that it was to be used *only* for her grandmother to make a sweater for herself—and not anyone else!

Susan was standing over the straw basket in which the yarn was displayed, trying to figure out how much to buy, when a woman wearing a name tag that said Betty came over to her. Smiling, she said, "You look a bit confused. Is there something I can help you with?"

"Yes, there is, as a matter of fact," Susan replied with a chuckle. "I'd like to get enough yarn for my grandmother to knit a sweater for herself, but I don't know how many skeins to get."

"How big is your grandmother?" Betty asked.

"Not very big. Probably about your size. You may even

know her since she lives right around here. She's Emily Pratt, who lives right here in Ridgewood."

"Of course I know Emily!" the woman who owned the craft supplies store exclaimed. "Why, she's in here all the time buying things for her craft projects. She's so good at making things, isn't she? And I have a feeling that she'd love that yarn. Here, let me figure out how much she'll need. . . ."

While the woman rang up the yarn, Susan wandered around the store. Besides the yarn and fabrics and paints, there were some sample items on display, things that had been made out of the supplies that were for sale. There was a pastel patchwork baby quilt, a handknit vest made out of a dozen bright colors, some pieces of pottery that had been fashioned from a special kind of clay sold in the store.

As she picked up her package at the front of the store, she commented, "These are such pretty things! Who made them?"

"I did," Betty said, a little bit shyly. It was obvious that she was pleased by the compliment, however.

"Are they for sale?"

"Oh, no! I just make them for fun, then put them on display so the customers can see what the supplies I sell might be used for."

"Maybe you should open a gift shop as well!" Susan said with a smile as she headed out the door. "I'd be your very first customer!"

When she was out on Ridgewood Street once again, Susan looked at the clock on the church steeple and saw that she had been out shopping for almost two hours. She had promised to spend at least part of the afternoon helping her grandmother address last-minute Christmas cards, but there was still one more stop she wanted to make.

She had noticed that even though there were signs of the

holidays all over her grandparents' house, there was one thing missing: candy canes. She wanted to get some to put on the tree and tuck into Christmas stockings. After all, it just wasn't Christmas without candy canes! And so she stopped in at the small supermarket, hoping she could find a large bag of them.

Sure enough, there was a big display of candy canes right inside the door. Susan picked up a bag and headed for the cash register. As she was on her way, however, she noticed that someone else was also heading in that same direction.

"You go first," she said, stepping aside. "You got here ahead of me."

"No, that's all right. I'm in no hurry. . . . Why, it's you! Susan, isn't it? Susan Pratt? The girl with the red scarf?"

Susan noticed then that the boy beside her was Brian. She was surprised to be running into him again so soon. Even more than that, however, she was surprised by how pleased she was to see him.

"That's me!" she said. "Hi, Brian. Have you and Danny been building any more snowmen this morning?"

She expected him to smile. Instead, he suddenly looked very serious. "No, I'm afraid not. Danny had to go back to the hospital."

"The hospital! What hospital? Is he sick?"

"Unfortunately, little Danny is quite sick. He's a patient at the Ridgewood Children's Hospital, over on the other side of town. You've heard of it, haven't you?"

Susan shook her head. "No, I haven't. I had no idea there was a hospital in Ridgewood."

"Well, there is. I work there part-time to help pay my college expenses." Brian frowned. "Unfortunately, at the rate things are going, the hospital might not be around very much longer."

"What do you mean?"

"It looks as if it might have to close. That's going to mean trouble for an awful lot of people around here. You know, a lot of people in Ridgewood work at that hospital. Probably even more than are involved in the tourist trade.

"And then there are the kids. It's the only children's hospital around, and I'm afraid that, from now on, kids who get sick are going to have to go all the way to Montpelier for treatment."

Brian shook his head sadly. "As it is, a lot of these kids already live pretty far away from here. Like Danny, for instance. He came here from a farm in a tiny town about fifty miles away to get his broken arm set after he fell out of a tree. They found out he was also badly anemic, and now he's going to have to spend the entire week before Christmas in the hospital, away from his family. They can't come visit him every single day. And while I'm sure they'll make it up for Christmas Day, they'll only be able to stay for a few hours. Besides, what about Christmas Eve?"

As Susan waited for the cashier to ring up her purchase, she thought about what Brian had just said. Suddenly things were snapping into place. So Danny wasn't his brother, he was a patient at the hospital at which Brian worked part-time. The two of them had gone out just for the morning— to cheer the sick little boy up, no doubt. And that explained why poor Danny was longing for a "real Christmas"!

Once Brian had paid for the sugar, flour, and spices he was buying, and he and Susan were walking out of the store together, she said, "Well, at least Danny has you. And a place like a children's hospital must have all kinds of things going on around Christmas to keep the kids' spirits up."

"That's just the problem! They don't—at least not this year. It seems that the hospital is really short of funds all of a sudden. That's why it might have to close. And so the very first thing to go has been all the extras like presents for the kids and decorations and parties. Those of us who really care about the kids have been doing our best to cheer them up, but there's only so much we can do. . . ."

All of a sudden Brian looked over at Susan. "Hey, what am I doing, dumping all this on you? You don't even live around here, so what do you care about my problems?"

"But I *am* interested!" Susan protested, meaning what she said. "Really!"

"Aw, you're just saying that to be polite. Here you are, spending your vacation in this scenic little town of ours, and I'm probably ruining everything.

"But listen: I just had an idea, something for later on. I really can't talk now, because I have to get home to deliver this stuff to my sister." He held up the bag of things he'd just bought at the supermarket. "She's baking about six million different kinds of Christmas cookies this afternoon. I shouldn't complain, since she's a great cook and she always lets me sample as many as I want. But I do have to get going. . . . Anyway, how about going for a sleigh ride with me tonight? The chamber of commerce has got a bunch of those old-fashioned horse-drawn sleighs, and tonight's the first night they're getting them all set up. . . ."

"I'd *love* to!" Susan cried, thinking of the Christmas card that just two weeks ago had first inspired her and her sister to daydream about spending the holidays in a picturesque New England town. "It sounds like the perfect way to end my first real day of Christmas shopping!"

"Great!" said Brian. "I'll stop by around eight to pick you up, okay?" He grinned, then added, "When you invited Danny and me over to your grandparents' house, I'll bet you never expected to get such a quick response!"

Susan just laughed.

They had reached the Pratts' house by then. Susan was

sorry that Brian had to rush off, but after all, she would be seeing him again later on that same day. As she tromped through the snow on the lawn up to the front porch, she watched him disappear down one of the counry lanes that led off Ridgewood Street.

Even though she had a full afternoon ahead of her, addressing Christmas cards and chatting with her grandmother, she was already looking forward to that evening. And she had a feeling that the chance to ride in an oldfashioned horse-drawn sleigh was only part of the reason she was suddenly counting the hours until nightfall.

Four

While Susan was busy downtown, exploring Ridgewood, becoming friends with Brian, and learning about the problems that the children's hospital was having, Chris was practicing her jumps and turns on Maple Tree Pond, a good-sized body of water down the road from her grandparents' house. She had always enjoyed ice-skating, and over the years she had become an excellent skater. This was her first time out this season; even so, within only a few minutes it all came back to her. She sailed around the ice with ease, trying out her favorite moves and discovering that they were only a little bit rusty.

Her skill on the ice did not go unnoticed either. As she was just skating along, catching her breath after trying a leap that she had learned for the very first time only the year before, she suddenly became aware that someone was skating alongside her, a bit cautious and off-balance but nevertheless matching her stride.

Even before she looked over to see who it was, she heard a cheerful voice say, "Wow! Your grandparents told me a lot of nice things about you, but they never mentioned that you were an ice-skating champion!"

"Hi, Andy!" Chris said with a chuckle. "I'm far from a champion! But I do enjoy skating."

"Well, it shows. Mind if this amateur joins you for a quick spin around the pond?"

"Not at all. In fact, I'd be honored to skate with an actual resident of the state that's practically the country's headquarters for winter sports!"

"Even one who'd much rather be *inside* on a cold day like today?" Andy joked. "Or at least watching *other* people skate?"

"If that's the case," Chris returned, "then I'll just have to do my best to change your mind about the great outdoors!"

Their arms crossed and both hands held, professional figure skater-style, Andy and Chris skated together for a while, talking and laughing and having a wonderful time. She tried to show him how to do some fancier maneuvers, but Andy insisted that he was much better off when he stuck to the basics. Even so, the two of them had a lot of fun as she demonstrated some of the simpler moves and Andy made an effort to copy her—more often than not stumbling and falling, probably more because he was laughing so hard than anything else.

It wasn't long before he insisted that he had to go, however.

"But you've only been out on the ice for a few minutes!" Chris protested, following him off the ice onto the banks of the frozen pond. "Your nose isn't even red yet!"

"When you were born and raised in Vermont the way I was," Andy teased, "your nose *never* gets cold!" He sat down on a log and began to unlace his skates. "Actually, I'd really like to keep skating with you, especially since after about another twenty minutes with you as my teacher I'd probably be ready for the Olympics. But the truth is, I've got a million things to do today. Don't forget that Christmas is just a few days away!"

"In that case, I'm pleased that you decided to take out some time for some ice-skating."

"To be perfectly honest, I came here because your grandmother told me this was where you'd be." Andy grinned ruefully. "It's a good thing you weren't out skiing! I'm even worse at skiing than I am at ice-skating!"

"Oh, you're not such a bad skater," Chris countered, not certain of how to respond to his offhanded comment about how he had gone out of his way to seek her out. "With a little practice . . ."

"Okay, then, I'll make a deal with you." Andy slid off one skate, then the other, then tied their laces together in a square knot. "I wanted to find you so I could ask you to go on an old-fashioned sleigh ride with me tonight. It should be terrific. First a ride through this quiet little village of ours on a cold winter night, complete with horse-drawn sleighs, jingle bells, and the singing of Christmas carols. And then a big gathering in the community room, over at the church, with all the hot cider you can drink."

"It sounds great. . . ."

"But here's the deal. I promise that if you agree to go with me, I'll let you drag me out onto the ice for another lesson any time you please."

"Okay!" Chris replied with a chuckle. "But are you sure I can't talk you into going skiing instead?"

Andy groaned loudly. He pretended to start running away, toward the road.

"Save me!" he called in mock fear. "This girl will have me getting frostbite by the time she's through with me!"

Still hurrying away, he yelled over his shoulder, "Listen, Chris, I'll come by for you at eight. And take my advice:

Dress warmly! You may not have noticed, but it's *cold* up here in Vermont!"

It wasn't until early that evening that Susan had a chance to tell Chris what she had found out that afternoon about the problems that the Ridgewood Children's Hospital was having.

The two girls were getting dressed for the sleigh ride. Chris was in her bedroom, putting on so many layers of clothing that she could hardly bend her arms and legs. When Susan came into the room just before eight o'clock, she started to laugh.

"*Now* who looks like a snowman!"

Chris turned and saw that her sister was wearing only a jacket, hat, and mittens. Susan was right; by comparison, she *did* look a bit silly.

"I was warned that it gets pretty cold up here at night," Chris replied matter-of-factly. "But maybe I *am* overdoing it. . . ."

"Just a bit," said Susan. "I really do think that three sweaters are too many."

"Okay, then." With great relief, Chris pulled two of her sweaters off over her head. "There. Now I look like a person again instead of a snowman."

"Speaking of snowmen," Susan went on, suddenly serious, "something interesting happened to me today."

"Does that something interesting have anything to do with the boy who's taking you to the sleigh ride tonight?" Chris teased.

"As a matter of fact, it does. I met Brian while I was in town today. But meeting him was the good part of my little shopping spree. The bad part is something he told me about a children's hospital that's right here in Ridgewood, over on the other side of town."

She proceeded to fill her in on all the details of the Ridgewood Children's Hospital—at least, the little she knew about its current problems. She told her what having the place close down would mean to the town's residents, not to mention all the children who lived in the area. And that it was all because of a sudden lack of funds—something that sounded very mysterious, at least to her.

"But wait—that's not all of it," Susan went on after her sister had agreed with her that it was, indeed, a terrible situation. "Whether the hospital ends up closing or not, the fact remains that the children who'll be spending Christmas there this year are going to have a pretty dreary holiday. Brian says there's simply no money for things like decorations and parties, not to mention presents for the kids."

"Oh, no! That's just *awful,* Sooz! It sounds as if those poor kids aren't going to have any kind of Christmas at all! As if it weren't hard enough already, just being stuck in a hospital over the holidays, far away from their families and their homes. . . ."

"It doesn't seem fair, does it?" Susan sighed loudly. "If only there were something we could do . . ."

But before she and her twin had a chance to try to come up with some ideas, they heard their grandmother calling upstairs to them.

"Christine! Susan! Come on down. There are two young men here to see you."

Susan and Chris grabbed their things and scrambled down the stairs. It was time for the first horse-drawn sleigh ride they'd ever been on in their lives, and for the moment at least, that was all that mattered.

As they reached the bottom of the steps, the girls were so busy thinking about the evening ahead that they forgot all about the fact that Susan's date was unaware of one simple fact about the girl he was about to go out with for the very first time.

"Susan," Brian said nervously, "Is there . . . are you . . ."

Susan stood at the base of the stairs, just staring at Brian for a few seconds. And then she realized what he was talking about. She began to laugh.

"I guess I forgot to tell you, Brian, that my sister, Chris, and I are identical twins."

He immediately relaxed. "Gee, for a minute there I was wondering if I was . . ."

"Seeing double, right?" Andy chuckled. "You're not the first person to have that reaction, I'm sure. You know, you two should warn people that there are two of you!"

"Sometimes we forget," Chris said with a smile. "After all, Sooz and I are *used* to the fact that there are two of us!"

It was then that she noticed that her grandparents were wearing their coats as well.

"Are you coming, too?" she asked them hopefully.

"We certainly are!" John Pratt replied merrily. "Believe it or not," he added with a teasing wink, "we old-timers have never been on a horse-drawn sleigh ride before either. They'd already invented *cars* when we were young!"

The sleigh ride turned out to be exactly the way the girls hoped it would be. It was a beautiful night, not too cold and not at all windy, with the black winter sky made friendly by a shining yellow moon and a thousand twinkling stars. As the dozen or so horse-drawn sleighs made their way through the snow-covered winding roads of Ridgewood, their jingle bells a merry accompaniment to the Christmas carols that the gleeful passengers were singing, Chris and Susan both felt as if finally they were living in that Christmas card they'd both liked so much.

Just as Andy had promised, there was a large gathering at

the church right after—not only the people who'd been on the sleigh ride but dozens of other people from the town, as well, all packed into the church's community room. Recordings of Christmas carols were playing in the background and although they may have sounded more polished than the renditions just given by the sleigh riders, they were definitely no more heartfelt. There were decorations everywhere—wreaths and pine garlands and even a big Christmas tree decorated with lights and gingerbread boys and girls just like the ones that Susan had baked. In the middle of the room there was a huge punchbowl filled with hot mulled cider.

"Cider!" Susan exclaimed. "Just the thing to warm me up. Come on, Chris. Let's go get some. Besides, I see someone over there that I'd like you to meet."

She had recognized the woman standing next to the punchbowl sipping a mug of hot cider and talking to some of her friends as Betty, the owner of the craft supplies store.

"Excuse me," Susan said, going over to her with her sister in tow. "I don't know if you remember me. . . ."

"Well, of course I do! You're Emily Pratt's granddaughter, aren't you?"

"Yes, I am. Susan Pratt. And this is my twin sister, Chris." Turning to Chris, she explained, "Betty's is the shop where I got that pretty yarn for Grandma's Christmas present. You should see her store. It's filled with beautiful crafts that she's made. Just like the things that Grandma makes."

After Chris and Betty had chatted for a while, then said good-bye, Chris took Susan aside.

"Sooz, I'm a little confused. Betty is certainly very nice, but why was it so important to you that I meet her?"

"Well, Chris, I've been thinking. All through the sleigh ride, even though I was having a great time, I couldn't help worrying about that children's hospital I told you about. And at the same time I kept thinking about Grandma and Grandpa and how they want to sell the house and move down south. And, well, I decided that we simply have to do something about it."

Chris was suddenly interested. "And you've come up with an idea?"

"Well, no. Not exactly."

By now Chris was very confused. "But I don't understand. If you haven't come up with a plan, then what does Betty have to do with all this?"

Susan laughed. "To be perfectly honest, Chris, I'm not sure yet. But I'm working on it. And you know as well as I do that once one of us Pratt twins sets her mind to something, it's only a question of time before the wheels start rolling. . . ."

Chris laughed, knowing that what her sister had just said was perfectly true.

"But in the meantime," Susan went on, "let's get Grandma and Grandpa over here, along with Brian and Andy, and we can all have another mug of cider together. It's Christmas, and I want to make sure I spend as much time as I can with the people I really care about.

"After all," she added, with a twinkle in her brown eyes, "isn't that what Christmas is all about?"

Five

"*So, Sooz, what are you planning to do today?*" Chris asked her twin as she helped herself to a second serving of French toast and doused it with hot maple syrup.

"I haven't decided yet," Susan replied. "There are so many things to do here that I'm not sure where to start! I could go skiing or ice-skating or sledding or tobogganing. . . ."

It was early Monday morning, and the two girls were lingering over a leisurely breakfast. Even though this was a school vacation, they had found it impossible to sleep late. They were too anxious to have another day get under way.

"How about you, Chris? What are you going to do today?"

Chris shook her head slowly. "I'm afraid I've got to get some of my holiday obligations out of the way. Would you believe that I haven't done *any* of my Christmas shopping yet? I've got to start prowling around in those shops in Ridgewood, or I'm going to be caught empty-handed once the big day arrives!"

She stuck a forkful of French toast into her mouth. "I'm

not looking forward to this. I haven't got one single idea. . . ."

"Don't worry," her sister assured her. "Once you get going, between the cute little shops in Ridgewood and all the snow and Christmas decorations, I'm sure you'll get some inspiration!"

"I sure hope so." Chris sighed. "I'd much rather be in your shoes, trying to decide between skiing and ice-skating and sledding. . . ."

"I've got a better idea," a male voice suddenly boomed. "How about spending the morning taking the grand tour of the Ridgewood Children's Hospital, Susan?"

Surprised, Susan and Chris turned to see Brian Barker standing in the doorway of the dining room, wearing a shirt and tie underneath his moss-green wool sweater.

"Brian! What are you doing here?" Susan cried. "Especially so early in the morning. Why, it's not even eight-thirty yet!"

"I know," said Brian with a grin. "I'm on my way to work. And as I was leaving the house this morning, it occurred to me that you might enjoy taking a look around the hospital. Seeing where I work, meeting some of the kids, maybe even spreading around a little Christmas cheer."

"Gee, that sounds like fun," Susan said. "I'll go get my coat. Oh, and there's something else I want to bring along."

"Really? What's that?"

"Some Christmas cookies! If I know kids, that's one thing that will go a long way in spreading around some Christmas cheer!"

While Susan hurried into the kitchen to pack up some of the homemade cookies that she and her grandmother had baked, Chris and Brian chatted together in the dining room.

"You're welcome to join us, if you like," Brian offered congenially.

"Thanks, but I'm afraid I've got to get some Christmas shopping done." Chris made a face.

"It looks as if you dislike shopping as much as I do!" Brian laughed.

"Oh, it's not that. It's just that I don't have any ideas about what gifts to get. And frankly, I'm afraid that the selection in a small town like Ridgewood is going to be pretty limited."

"I know what you mean. That's a problem that a lot of us have." Brian shrugged. "What I always do is drive out to one of the malls around here. But I'm one of the lucky ones since I have a car. Old and beat-up, maybe, but a car nonetheless. I can't help wondering what everybody else does about that. Like older people and the mothers of small children. Sometimes the snowy weather around here makes for some pretty rough traveling, and it must be hard for them to get out to do their Christmas shopping."

Susan reappeared then, wearing her coat and carrying a big tin of cookies.

"Gee, the kids will really appreciate this!" Brian said warmly as he led her out to his car.

"Actually, *they're* doing *us* a favor!" She laughed. "We've got so many cookies that we'd never get rid of them all without some help! And if we did, we wouldn't be able to fit into any of our clothes anymore, because we'd all be shaped like Santa Claus!"

As Brian and Susan rode through Ridgewood toward the children's hospital, he told her a little bit more about himself. He was a freshman at the state university nearby, majoring in computer science and working in the hospital's computer center whenever he wasn't in class or studying.

"Gee, it sounds pretty exciting," Susan observed.

"Knowing a lot about computers, using it to help patients get the best medical care possible . . ."

"Actually, my work at the hospital is pretty straight-forward. Routine, even. And to be perfectly honest," Brian added with a chuckle, "I spend more time working on the hospital's budget and sending out bills than getting involved with the actual patients!"

He grew more serious then. "But I do care about the kids. That's why I try to get out of my office into the wards as much as I can. You know, to spend time with the children, playing games with them, teaching them songs, helping make the time they're in the hospital pass a little bit more quickly—and a lot more pleasantly."

"That's really nice of you." Thoughtfully, Susan added, "I wonder if I could get some of those kids interested in some art projects. I do have some experience in that area. . . ."

Brian brightened. "Really?"

Susan told him about her longtime interest in art, the classes in painting and drawing she was taking at school, her experience as an arts and crafts counselor at Camp Pinewood the summer before—and her dream of going to art school after graduating from high school.

"In that case," he teased, obviously impressed, "I'm definitely going to draft you into spending some time with the kids. I hardly even know how to hold a paintbrush much less teach a bunch of children how to make things out of paste and crayons and colored paper! Now that's a *real* talent!"

Susan chuckled. "Brian, I'd be more than happy to help out!"

By then they had reached the Ridgewood Children's Hospital, a redbrick building three stories high set behind a large circular driveway with a parking lot off to one side. It was a congenial-looking place except for one obvious fault.

There was not one single sign of Christmas.

"Gee, there isn't even a wreath on the front door," Susan commented with surprise as she and Brian strolled inside after he'd parked the car in a special section of the lot reserved for hospital employees. "I'm beginning to feel more and more sorry for the kids who are patients here every minute!"

"I know exactly what you mean," he agreed. "You'd think that this was Ebenezer Scrooge's house and not a hospital for sick children!"

Once inside, she was struck by how dreary the place looked. No Christmas tree, no decorations, not even any Christmas carols playing softly in the background.

Why, it's as if Christmas doesn't even exist! she thought sadly. The whole town is overflowing with decorations and carols and holiday cheer, yet anyone inside these walls would never even guess that today is December 20!

"Come on downstairs, and I'll show you where I work." Brian grinned ruefully as he pushed open a door near the front entrance that led to the stairs. "Unfortunately, they've got us computer types stuck down in the basement, far away from all the action. The only consolation is that the director of the hospital has his office down there, too. Probably so the rest of us won't feel quite so bad!"

Sure enough, the area in which Brian worked was tucked away at the end of a long hall, isolated from the rest of the hospital. Even so, it was a busy place. Three computer operators were already working at their terminals, clicking away on the keys of their machines so fast that it almost looked as if their fingers weren't moving at all.

After meeting Carol, Brian's boss, as well as the other computer operators that he worked with, and then taking a quick tour of the facilities, he led Susan out into the hall again.

"I really shouldn't stay away too long," he said, "although later on today I'll make up all the time I miss. Even so, let's just hope I don't run into Mr. Stone as we're going upstairs, up to the wards where the children stay."

"Mr. Stone? Who's Mr. Stone?"

"He's the director of the hospital. See, that's his office over there, right across from the computer room."

"Oh, I see. And I take it he's not in favor of having the computer people doing volunteer work with the children on the side?"

"That's not exactly the problem. . . ." Brian frowned. "Let's just say that there's something . . . funny about him."

"Funny?" Susan blinked. "What do you mean?"

"I'm not sure, exactly. Sometimes he's quite friendly . . . but a lot of the time he really keeps to himself. And, well, I often get the impression that he doesn't really *care* all that much about what happens here at the hospital."

"Doesn't care? But that's impossible! I mean if he's the director . . ."

Brian shrugged. "I know it sounds odd. That's why I said I'm not exactly sure. But there's definitely something peculiar about Mr. Stone."

The elevator door opened, and Susan and Brian stepped inside.

"At any rate, let's not worry about this now. You're about to meet some of the most terrific kids you've ever met in your entire life, and I don't want anything to spoil it!"

Brian's promise turned out to be one hundred percent accurate. Susan spent the next two hours in the company of some of the liveliest, spunkiest, most fun-loving children she had ever met. Even though every one of them was sick, they all seemed determined not to let that stand in their way.

A few were bedridden, and Susan and Brian stopped off to chat with each of those who were immobile. As for the others, however, they excitedly gathered together in the sun-room, pleased to have something different to do. Brian told them stories and played games with some of them. Susan, meanwhile, raided the hospital's limited supply of colored paper, paints, and crayons and showed the children how to make paper wreaths and stars to decorate their rooms, as well as the rooms of those who weren't well enough to create their own.

When she and Brian finally dragged themselves away and were walking down the stairs back to the computer center, Susan discovered that there were tears in her eyes.

"What's wrong?" Brian asked, concerned.

"Oh, nothing." she sighed deeply. "It just doesn't seem fair, that's all. I mean, those kids are so great . . . yet they're hardly having any Christmas at all."

"Yeah, I know," Brian agreed sadly.

However, while he was dwelling on how unjust the whole situation was, Susan's mind was clicking away, plotting and planning and searching for a solution. Now that she had met the patients of the Ridgewood Children's Hospital, witnessed their charm and their determination firsthand, she wanted more than ever to recruit her sister and do something to help.

I have absolutely no intention of letting those kids' Christmas pass by without some fanfare, she thought with resolve. At least, not as long as Susan and Christine Pratt possess a single ounce of yuletide spirit!

Six

"Grandma, these are beautiful!" Chris squealed. "Did you really make them?"

It was Monday afternoon, just after Chris had returned empty-handed from her morning of Christmas shopping. She came home discouraged, convinced that she would never find the right gifts for her sister and her grandparents in a town as small as Ridgewood. In an attempt to cheer her up, her grandmother had suggested that the two of them do some exploring.

Now Chris and Emily Pratt were up in the attic's storage room, right behind the two bedrooms that the twins were using, rummaging through the old trunks and hatboxes and cardboard cartons that were stored up there. There were mostly old discarded things packed up in those boxes: well-worn clothes that were no longer in style or that didn't fit anymore; a set of dishes, many of them chipped, that had once been much loved but had since been replaced by a newer set; photographs and letters that had been lovingly tied up with ribbons and put in boxes, then left upstairs where they would be safe.

But Emily Pratt had also tucked away some of her handmade craft items. Some of them were projects that were only half finished, sweaters she planned to finish knitting when she had the time, a yellow and blue hooked rug she hoped to go back to after the holidays when things quieted down once again. But the two patchwork quilts that she had just unfolded were indeed completed, and as Chris had noted with such enthusiasm, they were quite beautiful.

"Yes, of course I made them!" Emily Pratt said with a laugh, blushing with pleasure over her granddaughter's reaction to the handmade creations, looking on proudly as Chris admired the two quilts.

One of them, made up of a dozen different light blue fabrics, was the L-shaped patchwork design called Log Cabin. The other, made in pinks and greens, was the pretty Ohio Star pattern. Both had intricate handwork, with each and every patch outlined in small, even stitches, and it was evident that they were not only expertly done but had required long hours of demanding work.

"One of these quilts is for you, and one is for Susan. You two can decide who likes which one of them better. I made them for you girls to use when you have homes of your own. After all, next year you'll both be going off to college, then living on your own after you graduate, getting jobs and having your own apartments. . . ."

The older woman's eyes filled with tears, as if just thinking about the rapid passage of time made her sad. Chris noticed immediately. She put the quilts down, then went over and threw her arms around her grandmother.

"Oh, Grandma, sure Susan and I will grow up and do those things one day. But what about *right now*? We're all together, you and me and Grandpa and Sooz, for the first time in years. And it's so great to see you both again! Let's concentrate on the present and make sure we have a wonderful time!"

Emily Pratt dabbed at her eyes and nodded. "You're right. I should be thinking about the present, and how lovely it is to see you girls once again. Just having you both here has already made this the merriest Christmas that your grandfather and I have had in a very long time!

"And do you know one thing that's really struck me during this visit?" she added, her dark brown eyes suddenly twinkling.

Chris shook her head.

"How much you both remind me of your father when he was your age!"

"Really?" Chris laughed. "It's hard to imagine Daddy *ever* being our age. . . ."

"Well, he certainly was! He looked a lot like the two of you, but you three have got other things in common as well. You know, he was quite a prankster, just like you girls. Wait, let me get out some of those old photographs." Emily surveyed the attic storage room for a few seconds, her face lighting up once she spotted a huge photograph album sitting on top of a pile of folding-lawn chairs being stored up in the attic over the winter. "Why, I remember one time when he was just about your age. . . . He and his best friend—Skip, I think his name was—decided to start a part-time business after school, doing odd jobs and washing cars and mowing lawns. . . . But they didn't own a lawn mower, so they had to come up with a way to borrow one. . . ."

For the next hour and a half, Emily Pratt enthralled Chris with tales of her son, the twins' father, when he was a teenager, making her stories come alive with the photographs that lined the pages of the thick leather-bound album. The younger Pratt couldn't hear enough about the young man who had gained a reputation as Ridgewood's resident mischief maker, always coming up with some scheme or another, more often than not ending up by laughing at the way that things turned out but having fun anyway.

Chris was also glad that her grandmother seemed to be having such a good time reminiscing about bygone days. For a while at least she forgot all about her contention that she and her husband were too old to hold on to the house, that it was time for them both to move to a retirement village. Instead, she allowed herself to be the vibrant, fun-loving woman she really was—getting on in years, perhaps, but nevertheless as young at heart as she had always been.

As she snapped the photograph album shut, declaring with a chuckle that she was getting hoarse from talking so much, Emily caught sight of her wristwatch.

"My goodness, just *look* at the time!" she cried. "Why, we've been up here in this dusty old attic for hours! You should be outside, Christine, skiing or skating or whatever, breathing our fresh country air. And I should be thinking about getting dinner started. Why, I've whiled away almost the entire afternoon strolling down Memory Lane!"

"But it's been such fun," Chris said sincerely. "I can go ice-skating any time, but it's not very often that I get to spend the afternoon with one of my favorite people in the whole world!"

She hugged her grandmother, then the two of them started putting away the boxes and photographs they had been having so much fun looking through. As they were getting ready to go back downstairs once again, Chris noticed a big straw basket that had been hidden behind an old bicycle. In it were all kinds of small handicrafts made out of gay fabrics, a collection of bright colors and patterns that immediately made her curious.

"Oooh, what's that, Grandma?" Chris couldn't help peeking inside.

"Just some more things I made." Emily Pratt shrugged. "I so enjoy making things that sometimes I make them just for the fun of it, without really intending to *use* them for anything in particular. Oh, I'll probably give them away one of these days as gifts. In fact, if you see anything you like, Christine, feel free to help yourself."

Chris looked through the contents of the big basket, filled with awe. There were all kinds of things, each one beautiful and bright and carefully made. Patchwork potholders, little baskets made out of yellow calico, small stuffed animals, pincushions, even doll clothes. She was amazed.

"Grandma, these things are incredible! Did you ever think of selling them?"

Emily Pratt waved her hand in the air and pretended to scowl. "Oh, it would be too much trouble finding a store that would carry my things, worrying about whether people would like them enough to buy them. . . ."

"How could anyone *not* like them?" Chris demanded. "You can make so many different kinds of things, and each one is wonderful in its own way!"

"Why, thank you for the compliment, Chris. I'm pleased that you like them so much. But well, the truth is that most people find it easier just to go to one of the local malls and buy things there. You know, things they've seen advertised in magazines, names they're already familiar with, rather than buying handmade things. I suspect they're just not used to it.

"Besides," Emily went on, "a lot of my friends make things of their own. And since they're the kind of people who appreciate handcrafted items enough to want them in their homes, there go my potential buyers!"

She laughed to herself. "Now, Christine, why don't we

go downstairs and have a nice hot cup of tea? I don't know about you, but I need a rest after digging around in that musty old attic all afternoon!"

"Sure, Grandma," Chris agreed. "That's a great idea."

But as she accompanied her grandmother down the stairs to the kitchen, Chris was lost in thought. And there were two separate issues on her mind. One was the beautiful handicrafts that her grandmother was so good at making—and her contention that no one would ever be interested in buying them to brighten up their own homes. The other was her plan to move south because she felt that she and her husband were old-timers now, a belief that contrasted so strongly with her lively spirit and her love of being busy and involved in things. Neither of them made any sense . . . and Chris was unable to forget either of them. She was just too troubled by them both.

I think it's time for Sooz and me to have a heart-to-heart talk, Chris was thinking as she bounded down the last few stairs ahead of her grandmother, anxious to get to the kitchen first so she could make the tea. There's one thing that's becoming more and more clear to me every day: Sooz and I have *definitely* got our work cut out for us!

Later that afternoon when Susan arrived home after her day at the Ridgewood Children's Hospital with Brian Barker, Chris was all set to talk to her. But before she could say a word, her twin, still wearing her coat, her nose and cheeks still red from the cold, found her upstairs in her bedroom and declared, "Chris, you and I have got to have a talk!"

Chris's mouth immediately dropped open. "Sooz, that's exactly what *I* was going to say! I think you and I must be on the same wavelength!"

"I don't know about that. Because what I've got to say is

something that you probably haven't been giving very much thought to all day."

Susan, obviously very excited, took off her coat, kicked off her shoes, and plopped down on Chris's bed, taking care not to muss up the yellow patchwork quilt that was serving as its bedspread. "But *I* certainly have. Chris, I just had the most amazing day over at the Ridgewood Children's Hospital! You should see that place! The kids there are great! I mean, most of them are having a really tough time, being sick and stuck in a hospital and all. . . . And of course it's even worse than usual now that it's Christmastime. But they're all so spunky and cheerful, as if they're determined not to let being in the hospital during the holidays get them down."

"Good for them!" Chris interjected.

"Yes, but there's more. The hospital is low on funds. It's losing money, in fact. It might even have to close. But that means that there's practically no Christmas celebration going on at all! No decorations, no parties, no presents . . . not even a Christmas tree. Imagine! There are fir trees *everywhere* here in Vermont, yet those poor kids don't have a single Christmas tree in the entire hospital!"

"I think I can guess what you're going to say next," said Chris with a chuckle as she sat down on the bed beside her sister. "You want to do something to help the children at the Ridgewood Children's Hospital have a merry Christmas, right?"

Susan looked at her in amazement. "Why, Chris! How on earth did you know?"

Chris burst out laughing. "Let's just say that I know you pretty well. Besides, I must confess that I've been thinking kind of the same thing."

She told her twin all about the afternoon she had spent with her grandmother, talking to her about the past and looking at all the beautiful handicrafts she had made, including some that she'd made just for fun without having any real use for them.

"And I feel just as committed to helping Grandma and Grandpa realize that they'd be lost if they sold their house and moved and that they're both very involved in so many of the things that keep people young—work they enjoy, hobbies they love, reaching out to other people—as you do to helping the children at the Ridgewood Children's Hospital," Chris finished. "There must be *some* way . . ."

Susan shook her head slowly. "I know exactly how you feel, Chris. Deciding that you want to help someone out and knowing how to do it can sometimes be two very different things." She shrugged. "Oh, well. Enough about that for now. Tell me: How did your Christmas shopping go this morning?"

Chris groaned. "Terribly! I didn't buy a single thing for anybody! Oh, sure I saw some nice things in the little shops here in Ridgewood. But nothing seemed to be just right. Nothing I saw was distinctive enough . . . *special* enough for the people I care about." She sighed. "I don't know *where* I'm going to get Christmas presents this year!"

She looked over at her twin, expecting some advice or at least some sympathy. But Susan looked as if she weren't listening at all.

"Sooz, aren't you going to say anything?" Chris demanded. "I mean, here I am telling you all about what a hard time I've been having trying to get my Christmas shopping done . . ."

All of a sudden, Chris realized that her sister *was* listening to her. In fact, she was listening to every word she said with the greatest interest.

And the gleam in her eye told her that once and for all, Susan had come up with a solution. . . .

"Chris, I've *got* it!" she breathed, barely able to contain her excitement. "It's finally come to me! I've had a brainstorm . . . the answer to all our problems!"

"*All* our problems?" Chris asked doubtfully. "Not that I doubt your ingenuity, Sooz, but you've got to admit that we're dealing with some problems here that are pretty different from each other. . . ."

"It's the perfect plan!" Susan insisted. By now she was practically jumping up and down. "Listen to this, Chris. You and I will organize a Christmas bazaar! We'll get *everyone* involved! Grandma and Grandpa, Brian, Andy, even Betty from the craft supplies store. We'll sell handicrafts made by Grandma and her friends and home-baked Christmas cookies and . . . and Christmas trees, and all the profits will go to making a merry Christmas for the kids over at the Ridgewood Children's Hospital!"

"Sooz, that *is* ingenious!" Chris declared. "That way, we can help the children have a real Christmas!"

"That's right. And at the same time, we'll be helping convince Grandma and Grandpa that they're not too old to be much good for anything, or whatever it is they said about the way they've been feeling lately, because we'll get them both so involved in getting this bazaar off the ground that they'll realize that they really are still young at heart."

"That's right," Chris agreed. "And there's one more benefit, too: People like me who've had trouble with their Christmas shopping will have no problem at all finding wonderful things to buy there to give as gifts. Why, a bazaar like the one we're going to have is the answer to a Christmas shopper's dreams!"

"See?" Susan said, pretending to be smug. "My idea *is* the answer to all our problems!"

"I'll say! Why, it's a *fantastic* idea, Sooz. One of the best you've ever had!"

"Good, I'm glad you're in favor of it. After all, Chris, you and I will have to put in a lot of work between now and Christmas. Not only planning the bazaar, either. We'll also have to plan a way to help those kids at the hospital celebrate Christmas."

Chris nodded seriously. "I'm pretty sure we can get Andy and Brian to help us with the organizing. After all, they both know Ridgewood a lot better than we do, so they can help us pick out a place to hold the bazaar and give us some ideas on how to get the local people interested."

She paused for a moment, just thinking about all they would have to do in order to make their plan work. "Let's see, we'll need posters and tables and music. . . . Oh, dear, can we really *do* all this, Sooz? Christmas *is* only a few days away!"

"Of course we can, Chris! After all, we'll have lots of help. If we play our cards right, we can manage to get the whole town of Ridgewood behind us! Now today is Monday, and Christmas Eve is this Friday. If we have the bazaar on Thursday, we'll have all day Friday to plan a big Christmas Eve celebration for the kids at the hospital!"

"Thursday!" Chris groaned. "That means we only have tomorrow and Wednesday to get everything ready!"

Susan just grinned. "Come on, Chris. We can do it. After all, we Pratt twins have risen to greater challenges than this in the past, haven't we? And we've always managed to come out on top."

"I guess so," Chris agreed, enthusiastic once again. "But we'd better get going right away. Why don't we make a list of things we've got to do between now and Thursday, the day of the bazaar? Then we can decide what order to do them in. . . ."

"Right. And we can figure who we'll need to help us, too."

Susan went over to the dresser and got out a small spiral notebook and a pen. On the front cover of the notebook, she triumphantly wrote, "The First Annual Town of Ridgewood Christmas Bazaar."

"There!" she cried. "How's that for a name?"

"Perfect! Now let's see. We'll need a place to hold the bazaar, that's the very first thing. I bet Andy could help us out, or maybe Grandma and Grandpa will have some ideas about that. Then, once we've got that decided, we can start thinking about posters to advertise the bazaar. We can put them up all around town, in the windows of stores and on telephone poles. . . ."

"And you can design them!" Chris suggested. "You're so talented that you're the perfect person to be the bazaar's official artist!"

"Okay," Susan agreed. "I love doing things like that. As a matter of fact, I'll start designing a poster right away."

"Great. And in the meantime I'll talk to Andy about the best place to hold a Christmas bazaar."

"You know, Chris," Susan said thoughtfully, jotting down "Location" and "Poster" on her list, "I thought I was excited about the holidays before. But that was *nothing* compared to all the Christmas spirit I've got now!"

Seven

True to their word, Chris and Susan began working on the First Annual Town of Ridgewood Christmas Bazaar right away. And as in the case of almost everything else the twins embarked upon, they gave it not only every spare moment they had but every ounce of energy and creativity they had as well.

The very first step, as Chris had noted, was finding a place in which to hold the bazaar. As soon as she and her sister had finished writing up their preliminary list, she hurried downstairs to find someone who had lived in Ridgewood all his life, who knew every nook and cranny and all the ins and outs of living in the small Vermont town . . . and who would get just as excited over the prospect of a Christmas bazaar as the twins themselves.

Chris found Andy in front of the Pratts' house, shoveling that afternoon's light snowfall off the front walk. It was still snowing; fortunately, the flurries that were falling now, cascading gently over the town from the black winter sky, were disappearing the moment they touched the ground.

"Andy! Got a minute?" Chris called, throwing her wool

56

jacket over her shoulders and venturing out onto the porch as she called to the red-haired boy who was huffing and puffing as he worked efficiently at clearing the path connecting the house with Ridgewood Street.

He glanced up and grinned from ear to ear when he saw who it was who was calling to him.

"Hiya, Chris!" he yelled back with a friendly wave of his hand. "Looking for something to do? Grab a shovel. I could use some help!"

"Thanks but no thanks!" Chris returned with a chuckle. "Actually, I was wondering if you could help *me* out!"

"Sure, Chris. Anytime. Especially if it means I get to take a break from this drudgery!"

Cheerfully he gestured toward the front walk, by now almost competely clear of snow. Then he abandoned his shovel and strode up to the front porch, stomping his boots on the wooden steps in order to shake the snow off.

"Now what can I do for the town of Ridgewood's number-one tourist?"

"Funny you should say that. What I'm going to propose will hopefully raise me from the level of tourist to honorary citizen," Chris joked. More seriously, she added, "What would you say about an idea my sister and I just had that's guaranteed to help all the kids at the Ridgewood Children's Hospital have one of the merriest Christmases ever, convince my grandmother and grandfather that selling their house and moving south would be the biggest mistake of their lives . . . and give this town the biggest dollop of holiday spirit that it's ever seen?"

"Whoa!" Andy exclaimed. "All this sounds too good to be true! Let me in on this brainstorm of yours!"

Chris proceeded to describe the Christmas bazaar that she and her sister had envisioned. Andy nodded as he listened, as if he were already recognizing that such an event could, indeed, accomplish every one of those things that Chris had promised in her dramatic introduction.

Then, as she outlined all the work that would have to be carried out over the next forty-eight hours in order to ensure that the Christmas bazaar would be the success she wanted it to be, Andy listened with a serious expression on his face.

When she was done, he patted her shoulder in a brotherly fashion.

"Wow, Chris, that does sound like a great idea! And don't worry, you've come to the right place. If anyone can help you two out of towners get this thing going, it's Andy Connors, born and raised within these town limits. As for coming up with a place in which to hold the bazaar, I already have the ideal location in mind."

"Really?" Chris was relieved that Andy was as enthusiastic as she and Susan were—and that he was familiar enough with the town of Ridgewood to be able to help them get things organized.

"Sure. Remember the church where we had that little gathering after the sleigh ride last night? Well, that community room is your anwer. It's huge, it's easy for the people who live around here to get to, everyone knows where it is . . . and I'll bet we'll have no trouble getting permission to hold a bazaar there for a cause as good as raising money for the Ridgewood Children's Hospital!"

"Great!" said Chris. "That does sound like the best place to hold our bazaar. Now all we need is a volunteer to go over there—the sooner the better—to talk to whoever it is who grants permission for people to use that community room and reserve it for this Thursday."

She looked at Andy meaningfully. With a teasing tone, she went on to say, "My, my. Just look at the time. Why, it's almost six o'clock! Don't you have dinner break coming up at six, Andy?"

Andy pretended to grimace, then burst out laughing. "Okay, Chris. I'll do it. I'll go over to the church right now and find out if we can use the community room this Thursday. Even if it means missing out on your grandmother's world-famous pot roast, which she just told me she's making for dinner tonight . . ."

"Don't worry!" Chris assured him. "I'll make sure that Grandma puts aside an extra large portion for you. Let me know how it all works out. Oh, and good luck!"

With that, Chris rushed back inside the house and up the stairs to her sister's room. Susan was sitting at the big oak desk in her bedroom, putting the finishing touches on a poster that could easily be run off in Ridgewood's print shop so that there would be enough copies to put in store windows and on telephone poles all over town. There was a blank space at the bottom in which she planned to fill in the details about time and place once everything was set, but the rest of the poster was completed—and expertly done.

"Christmas Bazaar!" said the bold headline. In smaller print were all the other details, like the fact that the proceeds from the bazaar would go to provide a holiday celebration for the young patients at the Ridgewood Children's Hospital. In the margins of the poster were intricate illustrations, drawn by Susan with black india ink: a sprig of holly, a wooden rocking horse, three of Santa's elves painting the face on a rag doll.

"Oooh, Sooz, it's perfect!" Chris exclaimed, looking over her sister's shoulder as she drew in the curlicues on Santa Claus's beard. "That headline will really make people stop and read on. And those pictures you've drawn are guaranteed to put people in a Christmas mood!"

"I sure hope so," Susan said with a modest smile. "Now all we need is a place to hold this bazaar of ours!"

"Don't worry. I've already got Andy working on it. He's

pretty sure we can use the community room over at the church—you know, where the gathering was last night after the sleigh ride. Oh, Sooz, I can't believe that everything is already starting to fall into place! This bazaar is really going to happen, and it's going to be fantastic!"

"Well, so far so good, anyway." Susan, always a bit more reserved than her twin, remained more cautious about the prospects for the town bazaar—at least at this point. "We'll just have to wait and see if everything else works out the way we've planned. Don't forget: Even if we have a place to hold the bazaar and the posters that will hopefully get people to come, we have yet to plan the bazaar itself!"

Just then the girls heard their grandmother calling them downstairs to dinner. They scrambled toward the door of Susan's bedroom, anxious to tell their grandparents about their idea.

"We can tell Grandma and Grandpa all about the Christmas bazaar while we sample some of Grandma's famous pot roast," said Chris as she headed for the stairs.

Her sister looked puzzled. "Famous? I never heard of it before!"

"Well," Chris admitted, "to be perfectly honest, I never did either until just now. And that was only because I had some inside information!"

"I don't care if this pot roast is famous or not," Susan said with a laugh. "I'm so hungry that I'm even willing to eat food that *no one* has ever heard of!"

Chris and Susan never got a chance to surprise their grandparents with the news of their latest venture, however. As soon as they sat down at the table, John Pratt brought up that very subject.

"What's this I heard about a Christmas bazaar?" he asked with a twinkle in his eye as he reached for a slice of New

England brown bread, still warm, that Emily had taken out of the oven just a few minutes before.

"How did you know about that?" demanded Chris, so surprised by his question that her mouth dropped open.

"Easy," her grandfather replied. "Ridgewood happens to be a *very* small town. And in small towns, nothing remains a secret for very long!"

"Especially if some of the town's more distinguished citizens like to eavesdrop," Emily Pratt said, pretending to scold. "You girls should have seen your grandfather, standing next to the window by the porch, taking in every word Chris and Andy were saying to each other!"

"Grandpa, you didn't!" Susan cried. "How are Chris and I going to manage to keep any Christmas secrets if you're going to go around listening in on all our conversations?"

"I guess I'll just have to try to restrain myself," John Pratt replied. "Not that that's very easy to do around Christmastime, of course. But let's not get off the subject. If there's going to be a Christmas bazaar, I want to know about it. I'll be your very first customer! In fact, I'll be there the minute it opens!"

"You can do better than that," Susan countered with a mischievous smile. "You can help Chris and me make it happen!"

"You, too, Grandma," said Chris. "As a matter of fact, Sooz and I really need your help if this thing is going to come off at all!"

John and Emily Pratt exchanged wary glances.

"I don't know," Emily said slowly. "Don't forget that your grandfather and I aren't as young as we used to be. We don't have that much energy anymore. . . ."

Chris stifled her first impulse, which was to contradict her grandmother, to insist that she was just as lively as ever and that she was just feeling as if she should be slowing down because of what the calendar was telling her. But instead she said, "But Sooz and I are really counting on you two! After all, you've both lived here for so long that you know everybody in this town, and so you can help us convince them to volunteer to help us make the bazaar a success. Besides, you're both bound to come up with some good ideas, ones that Susan and I could never think of. . . ."

"Well, I guess we could help you girls out a little," John Pratt finally said. "Just tell us what we can do."

Over a delicious dinner of pot roast—so good that Chris was sure that it deserved to become famous if it wasn't already known throughout the state of Vermont—the girls told their grandparents all about their plans for the Christmas bazaar. There would be entertainment, they hoped, local people singing Christmas carols and playing musical instruments and doing whatever else they were talented in. But the main attraction would be booths—or, more likely, long lines of tables covered in red and green fabric tablecloths—displaying gift items, decorations, and edible goodies that people could buy, with the profits of course going to pay for the children's holiday celebration over at the hospital on Christmas Eve.

After they described the way they saw the bazaar, their grandparents were silent for what seemed an eternity.

And then John Pratt said, "You know, I'll bet we could make some money selling Christmas trees. After all, a lot of people wait until the last minute, then decorate their trees on Christmas Eve. Maybe Andy and I could go up to the woods tomorrow and cut down a few to be sold at the bazaar."

Chris and Susan looked at each other, their brown eyes shining.

"That's *exactly* the kind of ideas we need!" Chris exclaimed.

And it was not only the sale of Christmas trees to help raise money for the hospital that seemed like such a good idea to Chris. Having her grandfather go outside and cut down trees, just when he was feeling he was too old to be of any use to anyone, was precisely the kind of thing the twins had been hoping to get their grandparents involved in, to help convince them that they were still spirited and energetic . . . and young at heart.

"I have an idea, too," Emily ventured, setting down her fork thoughtfully. "You know I like to make things, and well, as Chris knows, I've got some things that I made just for fun that I'd be pleased to donate to the bazaar. I could spend all day tomorrow and Wednesday making some more as well—little things, like patchwork pillows and stuffed animals and potholders, out of the fabric scraps I've saved.

"And, come to think of it, if I make a few telephone calls this evening, I'll bet I could get some of my friends to donate some of the things that they've made, too. Why, Jean knits so quickly that I'll bet she could make two or three baby sweaters by Thursday. And Mary Evans is good with baskets; maybe I could talk her into parting with a few. Then there's Virginia, who makes pottery, and her husband makes toys out of wood. . . ."

She thought for a moment, then broke out into a huge smile. "Come to think of it, I could plan an entire bazaar myself, using just the creative people I know here in town!"

"Don't forget baked goods," Susan reminded her. "Perhaps some of your friends who aren't skilled at making crafts could make Christmas cookies for us to sell."

"Oooh, I have an idea!" Chris exclaimed. "Someone could make up one of those fancy gingerbread houses, decorated with cookies and candy and white icing that looks like snow, and we could raffle it off!"

Susan and her grandmother looked at each other and smiled.

"That sounds like an awful lot of fun," Susan said. "Do you think that between me planning the bazaar and you making fabric items to sell at it, you and I could find the time to make a gingerbread house? I've always wanted to try . . . and I've got a wonderful recipe for gingerbread dough. Why, I welcomed in the Christmas season this year by making little gingerbread people!"

"And they were fantastic," Chris said sincerely. "If you two want to volunteer to make the gingerbread house, the honor is all yours. We can place it right at the very front of the room so it's the very first thing that people see when they come into the bazaar."

"Okay, great!" said Susan enthusiastically. "And I just thought of someone else who can bake things for us to sell. Brian mentioned that he has a sister who likes to make cookies. I'll ask him to talk to her."

"Wow, this bazaar is already shaping up!" Chris exclaimed. "Now there's one more idea I had. While Grandpa is cutting down Christmas trees with Andy, and Sooz and Grandma are baking the gingerbread house, I can go around to the shops here in Ridgewood and ask the shopkeepers to donate things for us to sell. You know, the card store could donate Christmas wrapping paper and pretty stationery that people could give as gifts. Betty at the craft supply store might donate some yarn or some craft books. Then there's the bookstore. . . ."

"That's a lovely idea," said Emily. "And that way, everyone in town could get involved in helping raise money for the children's hospital. Not only by going to the bazaar but by helping make it happen in the first place."

"Whew!" Chris said suddenly. "We've certainly got our work cut out for us! Sitting around the dinner table and discussing all this is one thing. Going out and doing it is going to take a lot of footwork and coordination and creativity. . . ."

"But I think we can make it work," Susan insisted. "We've already got so many good ideas. And we *do* have two full days to get everything ready. . . ."

"Now all we need is a place to hold the bazaar!" Chris interjected ruefully.

Just then Andy strolled into the dining room, grinning from ear to ear.

"I take it you've got some good news for us," Susan said with a chuckle. "At least, if the expression on your face is any indication!"

"As a matter of fact, I have!" Andy declared. He sat down at the dining room table. "As far as the folks over at the church are concerned, we're on. We've got the community room all day Thursday and Thursday night as late as we please. Gee, so far everyone I've talked to thinks that holding a Christmas bazaar to raise money for the children's hospital is a great idea. And everybody wants to help!"

"It sounds as if Andy here has recruited some more volunteers for you girls," said Emily with a smile.

"As a matter of fact I have. Mrs. King, who plays the organ over at the church on Sundays, asked if we'd be interested in having her play Christmas carols on the piano during the bazaar. I don't know if you noticed, but there's a piano right in the community room. It was tucked away in the corner the other night, but I think having some music could add a nice touch.".

"Perfect!" Susan cried. "And if we do get some of the local people to volunteer to sing or perform, she can be their accompanist."

"Wait—there's more. Mrs. Washington, who made the

hot cider we were drinking last night, offered to make some for the bazaar. That way people can buy a cupful to drink while they enjoy the entertainment."

"And we can sell Christmas cookies and brownies and things for people to eat on the spot," said Susan. "Besides selling them by the batch for people to bring home, I mean."

"But wait—there's one more thing." Andy grinned. "I have a feeling you're going to like this one a lot."

"Things are going so well that I can't imagine what else you've got up your sleeve, Andy Connors!" Chris cried. "So you'd better end the suspense and tell us."

"Well, while I was over at the church talking to Mrs. King and Mrs. Washington, I ran into Mrs. Keating, the Sunday school teacher. She's got a class of seven-year-olds, and they've been rehearsing a little song and dance number just for the fun of it. All the boys and girls get dressed up like Santa's elves, and they bring in toys and pretend they're working at making them while they sing. It sounds pretty cute, and Mrs. Keating said the kids would be thrilled to perform at the bazaar. Especially since the whole idea of the bazaar is to raise money for kids like them who are sick and have the bad luck to be in the hospital over Christmas."

"You're right, I *do* like that one a lot!" said Chris. "Wow, this bazaar of ours is sounding better and better every minute!"

"Well, if we want it to be as good as it promises to be," said Emily Pratt, standing up from the table, "I'd better get on the phone and start talking to some of my more creative friends. And while I'm at it, I'd better check on my supply of sugar and flour and spices. Making a gingerbread house is no small task!"

"And I'd better go check on my electric saw." John Pratt stood up as well. "No time for dessert tonight. Andy, you'd better rest up. Tomorrow we're going to start cutting down some Christmas trees to sell at the bazaar. And, believe me, that's a lot more work than shoveling the front walk!"

"Okay, Mr. Pratt," Andy agreed cheerfully. "Sounds like fun. Just let me know when you're ready to go up into the hills."

"I guess I'd better get moving, too," said Susan. "Now that we're all set on the location for the bazaar, I can finish up that poster. Maybe I can even get it over to the printer's tonight so we can start putting them up all over town first thing tomorrow." She, too, stood up and left.

Now only Andy and Chris were left at the dinner table.

"Wow, you sure did a good job of getting everybody all fired up about this bazaar!" he exclaimed. "Maybe you should run for mayor in this town!"

"Maybe I will one of these days!" Chris countered.

"In the meantime how about keeping me company while I *finally* get to eat some of that pot roast that I've been thinking about ever since I left the church fifteen minutes ago? Planning Christmas bazaars is hard work!"

"Okay," Chris agreed. "But then I've got to run. I've got a million things to do. I've got to plan which stores to go to first tomorrow and decide the best way to lay out the tables at the bazaar and figure out the best way to get some of the local talent to perform. . . ."

"Whoa! You haven't even had dessert yet!"

"No time for that tonight. There's too much to do. Oooh, I'm so excited about this bazaar! It's funny how things work out, isn't it? Here Sooz and I vowed to help our grandparents feel young again while we were up here in Vermont, to come up with some way of making them feel vibrant and involved in things so that they'd reconsider their decision to sell the house. And Sooz wanted to find a way to help out

the kids at the Ridgewood Children's Hospital. . . ."
Chris sighed deeply. "And here it is, all about to happen!"

"It's about to happen, Chris, because you and Susan
decided that you wanted it to happen. That it was something
that you felt needed to be done. And you both deserve a lot
of credit for that!"

"Aw, shucks," Chris teased, trying to hide the fact that
she was blushing wildly at Andy's praise. "Now I'm going
to have just one more piece of that brown bread. After all, I
need to keep my energy up, or this bazaar will never come
off!"

As she lingered at the dinner table with Andy, downing
that one last piece of New England brown bread, it never
even occurred to Chris that in less than twenty-four hours, a
tremendous shadow would be cast over the holiday festivities that at this point she and the others were planning
with such optimism and joy.

Eight

"*How would you like to help the kids at the Ridgewood* Children's Hospital have a merry Christmas?"

It was the fifth time on that Tuesday morning that Chris had stopped into one of the stores on Ridgewood Street—and the fifth time that she had asked that question, one that the salesperson in her realized was a question that the shopkeepers of Ridgewood would have a difficult time saying no to. She had started out right after breakfast, armed with her notebook, in which there was a list of Ridgewood's stores; a pair of warm socks; and her biggest smile.

It was the first time she had ever done anything like this. And between her naturally outgoing personality and her commitment to making the Christmas bazaar the best it could possibly be, she was really enjoying talking about the idea she and her sister had developed as a way to raise money for a Christmas Eve celebration for the children who were in the hospital.

And that idea seemed to keep on growing. That morning as Chris was making the rounds, Susan was back at the house whipping up a tremendous batch of gingerbread dough, enough to build a spectacular gingerbread house and still have enough left over to make more gingerbread boys and girls and stars and bells to sell at the bazaar. John Pratt and Andy were up in the hills right outside Ridgewood, scouring the forests for fir trees that were suitable for selling at the bazaar as Christmas trees.

Emily Pratt, meanwhile, was driving around town, visiting each one of her friends. As she stopped at each house, she added to her car another box of handmade items that her fellow craftspeople were contributing to be sold, as well as enough secondhand items, clothes and toys and housewares that they no longer had any use for, to start up a white elephant sale table. She was also collecting red and green tablecloths to cover up the folding tables that Andy had promised to scrounge up, on which the items that were for sale would be displayed. And in the midst of all these activities, she was at the same time recruiting volunteers to help out, setting up and putting on price tags and selling the things that were being collected.

So far everything was going smoothly—including Chris's visits to all the shops in Ridgewood, where she was asking for donations. And this visit, at Shakespeare's Bookstore, was no exception.

"I'd be happy to donate some books for you to sell," said Dave Peabody, the proprietor of the shop, after Chris had explained all about the fund-raising bazaar. "I'll tell you what: I'll drop a cartonful of books by at the church first thing Thursday morning, before I open up the shop at nine-thirty. Will that give you enough time to set up the bookstall?"

"That would be perfect," said Chris with a nod. Inside her notebook, she made a note of the contribution that Mr. Peabody had just promised to make.

"And come to think of it, there's something else I can do to help out. I'd like to donate a few children's books, too, for you to give to some of the kids over at the hospital as Christmas presents. How would that be?"

Before Chris even had a chance to tell him what a terrific idea she thought that was, and how much she appreciated his generosity, Mr. Peabody went over to a display that was decorated with posters and clowns and ducks and cartoon characters and picked out six or eight different volumes, books for children of various ages and interests.

"Here you go," he said, putting them into a shopping bag and handing them to Chris. "Just tell the kids they're from Santa Claus," he added with a wink.

"Gee, thanks, Mr. Peabody!" Chris exclaimed as she took the bag. "I really appreciate these—and I'm sure the kids over at the hospital will, too!

"Now there's one more thing. Would you be willing to put a poster advertising the bazaar in the window of your store?"

"Of course!"

"That's wonderful, Mr. Peabody. I'll tell my sister, Susan, to stop in later on today to give you one. They're being run off at the printer's this morning."

"That's fine," said Mr. Peabody. "I'll tell you what: I'll even put it right smack in the middle of the window, where anyone walking by the shop will be sure to see it. Why, I think it may even fit right inside the wreath I've already got hanging in the window!"

Happily Chris left Shakespeare's Bookstore, pleased that she was now not only collecting donations for the bazaar and getting the shopkeepers to agree to display the poster that was already at the printer being run off, she was picking up gifts for the children as well. She couldn't wait to tell

Susan about how cooperative everyone in Ridgewood was being!

Gee, she thought with satisfaction as she tromped across the snow-covered sidewalk toward Betty's Craft Supplies, the next store on her list, getting everything ready for this Christmas bazaar is turning out to be more fun than I ever expected!

Mainly, she realized, because I'm beginning to see that I'm not the only one around here who's positively bursting with the *real* spirit of Christmas!

At noontime while Chris was still making the rounds at all the shops in Ridgewood's shopping district, Susan was heading over to meet Brian for lunch at the Ridgewood Children's Hospital in the car she had borrowed from her grandparents.

She had called him first thing that morning, but rather than telling him about the bazaar and the Christmas Eve party for the children at the hospital, she decided to tell him in person. So instead she simply said that she'd be stopping by to discuss something important with him and suggested that they meet for a sandwich in the cafeteria.

"Well, this is certainly a nice surprise!" Brian had said over the phone. "It's not often that I have a guest for lunch here at the hospital."

"Me inviting myself for lunch is nothing," Susan had teased. "Wait until you hear about the *real* surprise I'm going to tell you about!"

So Susan was excited as she hurried down the main corridor of the children's hospital toward the cafeteria. Not only would she be seeing Brian again, she couldn't wait to watch the expression on his face when she told him all her good news.

But as she spotted him sitting alone at a table near the

windows waiting for her, the expression on his face was positively gloomy. It was no secret that something was wrong—*very* wrong, as a matter of fact.

Even so, he cheered up as soon as he noticed Susan walking toward him.

"Hi, Susan!" he called. "And welcome to the town of Ridgewood's finest dining establishment!"

Susan chuckled as she looked around her at the small cafeteria, functional enough but definitely plain and cheerless, filled with hospital personnel: nurses and doctors in white, technicians and orderlies in green. They were all eating their lunches off plastic trays, using plastic silverware and paper plates and cups.

"This *is* an elegant restaurant," Susan quipped. "Unfortunately, it seems they've run out of linen tablecloths and candles and bouquets of flowers for decorating the tables. Perhaps we should look for the headwaiter."

"No matter," Brian returned with a lofty wave of his hand. "The fine food here speaks for itself. We don't even need candles and flowers." He stood up, bowed with mock formality, and offered her his arm. "Shall we?"

Susan giggled and took his arm. "Why, I'd be delighted!" With that, the two of them headed toward the cafeteria line.

A few minutes later, after Susan and Brian had returned to their table with their lunches, Susan said, "Well, Brian, I came here to tell you some good news. But to tell you the truth, when I walked into the room before, you looked as if you'd just lost your best friend."

The same troubled expression that she had seen on his face before returned. "Not quite. But I did just hear something that was pretty upsetting."

"Nothing's happened to any of the children, I hope. . . ."

"Oh, no, nothing like that." Brian frowned. "No, this has to do with the fact that the hospital has been losing money." Brian leaned forward so that he could speak more softly. "My boss, Carol, just told me that . . . well, it's really just a rumor, but . . ."

He looked around as if he wanted to make sure that no one besides Susan could hear him. "She said she heard that the reason the hospital is in such bad financial shape—so bad that it might even have to close down—is that the hospital's director has been embezzling funds."

"Mr. Stone?" Susan gasped. "Stealing money from the hospital?"

Brian nodded somberly. "I know. It's hard to believe, isn't it? As I said, it's only a rumor. But, gee, the very possibility that something like that might be going on . . ."

"Is there any way you could investigate?" asked Susan. By now she had forgotten all about her lunch, sitting on the plastic tray that she had pushed out of her way for the moment. "You know, find out whether it really *is* just a rumor? After all, that's a pretty serious accusation."

"I know it is. But to tell you the truth, I wouldn't have the faintest idea of how to go about something like that." He thought for a few seconds, then asked, almost as an afterthought, "Would you?"

But before Susan had a chance to answer his question, a voice that she didn't recognize boomed, "Well, hello there, Brian. Glad to see you're taking advantage of the hospital cafeteria's fine cooking. And who's your friend?"

Susan turned around and saw a distinguished man standing behind her, dressed in a well-cut suit. He had black hair that was peppered with strands of gray, a rather handsome face, and a way of carrying himself that bespoke confidence.

Brian gulped. "Hi, Mr. Stone. Susan, this is Mr. Stone,

the director of the hospital. Mr. Stone, this is Susan Pratt. She and her sister are spending the Christmas holidays with their grandparents, John and Emily Pratt, who live here in Ridgewood. . . ."

"How nice! I'm pleased to meet you, Susan. And welcome to the Ridgewood Children's Hospital. You know, it's not every day that a stranger stops in to take a look around."

What an odd thing to say! thought Susan. Aloud, she said, "Thank you, Mr. Stone." She glanced over at Brian, then boldly went on to say, "I'm particularly interested in your hospital because I understand that it's having some financial difficulties and that there isn't enough money for the children who are patients here to have much of a Christmas celebration." She watched his face carefully, anxious to observe his reaction.

But Mr. Stone simply said, "Yes, I'm afraid that's true. And I, for one, just couldn't be sorrier. These poor kids are having a rough enough time of it as it is, being stuck in the hospital over the holidays, without much of a chance to have a little holiday cheer."

"Gee, it's such an unfortunate situation," Susan agreed.

Goodness, maybe Mr. Stone is as upset about it as all the rest of us! Susan was thinking. He's certainly acting as if he is! It's difficult to believe that he could be responsible for the hospital's poor financial state, that he's the one who's keeping the kids from having a merry Christmas—who may, in fact, even be the reason that the hospital may have to close down soon!

"But things aren't entirely bad," she continued. "As a matter of fact, I was just about to tell Brian all about a plan my sister came up with to help the patients here have a holiday celebration after all."

"A plan? What plan?"

Susan couldn't help feeling that he was acting as if he were actually suspicious. But she went on to tell Mr. Stone, as well as Brian, all about the Christmas bazaar, the fund-raising event whose proceeds would be used to give the children at the hospital a Christmas Eve party, complete with decorations, music, cookies, and presents. When she finished her little speech, she looked from one of them to the other, anxious to see what their reaction would be.

She wasn't disappointed.

"Wow, that's a *great* idea, Susan!" Brian declared as soon as she'd finished.

"Yes, it is," Mr. Stone agreed, sounding sincere. "I'm sure the kids will love it—and the way you've described it makes it sound as if it won't cost the hospital a cent. I'm all for it. As a matter of fact, if there's anything that I or anybody else here at the hospital can do to help you out, just let me know. Why don't you contact my assistant, and the two of you can work out all the details? Brian here can give you the phone number. . . ."

Once Mr. Stone had moved on, apologizing for having to leave so quickly but insisting that he had some very important telephone calls to make, Susan turned to Brian and sighed.

"Well! Mr. Stone certainly seems like a nice fellow! I'm pleased he was so supportive when he heard about the party we're planning for the kids." She decided not to mention the reservations she already had about him based on those few rather peculiar comments he had made.

"Yes, he does seem nice, even if he does seem a little bit . . . withdrawn," Brian agreed. "That's why it's so darn hard to believe the rumor that Carol told me about." He thought for a few seconds, then said, "At any rate, there's nothing you and I can do about it, so why don't we forget it for now? I'd much rather hear more about the bazaar—and the party."

"Okay," said Susan, pulling her tray back and digging into her lunch. "The planning of the bazaar is already well under way—and in very good hands, I might add. But I'm sure you can give me some good ideas about the party. Things like the kind of refreshments the children might enjoy, games they'd have fun playing . . ."

"It sounds great, Susan, and I'd be more than happy to help you girls out in any way I can."

Brian seemed happier than she'd ever seen him as the two of them chatted away about the bazaar.

One thing's for sure, she thought, forgetting all about Mr. Stone for the moment. This bazaar is turning out to be an even better idea than I ever expected. *Everyone* is excited about it.

And knowing that made her realize that whether it turned out to be a success or not, she and her twin would have done their part to make this Christmas a merrier one for all the residents of Ridgewood.

As soon as she got home from having lunch with Brian at the hospital, Susan sought out her twin. She was anxious to hear all about how Chris's morning of soliciting contributions from Ridgewood's shopkeepers had gone before stopping off at the printer's to pick up the posters and start putting them up all around town. She also wanted to discuss the rumor that she had just heard from Brian . . . the one that was so difficult to believe.

She found Chris in the dining room with wrapping paper and ribbons and boxes spread out all over the table. She was humming, "Hark, the Herald Angels Sing" as she taped up the side of a large cube-shaped box she had just wrapped in shiny green paper.

"Well, well," joked Susan. "If it isn't one of Santa's elves."

"Not just any elf, either," Chris returned, looking up from her project and smiling. "You happen to be looking at Santa's *head* elf."

"In that case, I feel honored." Susan surveyed the generous stack of boxes placed on chairs, some of them already wrapped and decorated with ribbons in contrasting colors. "I guess you managed to do some Christmas shopping after all!"

"Oh, these aren't mine. They're Grandma's. She asked me if I'd help her out by wrapping them." Chris grinned at her twin mischievously. "If I'm not mistaken, I believe that one or two of these might even be for you!"

"Well, don't tell me which ones or what's in them. You know I always like to be surprised on Christmas morning."

Chris shook her head disapprovingly. "You were always so much more patient than I was. Here I was hoping I could talk you into peeking into some of these boxes with me. . . ."

"And spoil Christmas morning?" Susan laughed. "Never!" She grew serious then. "As a matter of fact, I've got something a lot more serious than Christmas presents on my mind right now. Can I talk to you for a minute?"

"Be my guest. But how about pitching in while we chat? Otherwise, I'll be up to my elbows in Scotch tape and ribbons all day!"

Susan picked up a long thin box from the pile and cut a piece of green paper, printed with silver bells, from a large roll. "You know I had lunch with Brian today . . . and he told me something awful, Chris. Of course, it *is* just a rumor . . . and one that's very hard to believe, at that."

Her twin's eyes grew round. "What is it, Sooz? It must be something serious, because you look pretty upset."

Susan sighed and ran her fingers through her short chestnut-brown hair. "Chris, Brian's boss, Carol, told him she thinks that the hospital's director, Mr. Stone, has been embezzling money from the hospital."

"The director? *Stealing?*" Chris was dumbfounded—so much so that she dropped the reel of red ribbon she had been holding, and it began to unravel as it rolled across the floor. "But . . . how . . . why . . ."

"That's exactly what *my* first reaction was," Susan said ruefully. "See, I told you it was hard to believe. And frankly, it's even harder now that I've actually met Mr. Stone."

"Really? You met him? What's he like?" Chris leaned forward excitedly. Suddenly it seemed as if there were something mysterious going on . . . and a mystery was something that she could never resist.

"Well, let me see." Susan thought for a few moments. "He did say a few things that were a little bit odd . . . but basically he's very nice. And he seemed genuinely upset that the hospital was so short of funds that it couldn't even manage a small Christmas celebration for the kids. Then when I told him about what we were doing, with the bazaar and all, he was delighted."

She frowned, then said, "I don't know, Chris. No matter what I felt about him personally, the fact remains that he *is* the hospital's director. So as far as I'm concerned, he's the *last* person I would ever expect to be doing something illegal. Not to mention something that could hurt the children at the very hospital he runs."

Chris abandoned her packages and began to pace around the dining room. "Boy, this is a real problem. Here the Ridgewood Children's Hospital is having financial trouble—may even have to close, in fact, something that would be bad for both the residents of the town and all the kids who live in this part of the state. It's an awful situation, and we both agreed as soon as we heard about it that we'd love to help out, if there was any way we possibly could.

"And then, out of the blue, we get some inside information on what may be the cause of all this. . . ."

"Wait a minute," Susan interrupted. "Inside information? I wouldn't go quite *that* far!"

"Well, maybe not. But, gee, Sooz, where's your sense of adventure?" Chris was suddenly excited. "Don't you see that this calls for some investigating, by a team of experts?"

Susan blinked as she looked up from the ribbon she was tying onto the package she had just wrapped. "*What* requires investigation, Chris?"

"Why, the possibility that Mr. Stone is the cause of the hospital losing money! I mean, you could look at it as only a rumor . . . or you could look at it as a lead."

Despite her twin's enthusiasm, however, Susan remained doubtful.

"But, Chris! We hardly have anything at all to go on! And besides, how could you and I possibly investigate something that's going on at the children's hospital? We don't even *belong* there, for goodness' sake! We don't work there, we don't do volunteer work there. . . ."

"No," said Chris, her brown eyes shining. "But we *are* giving a party there. On Christmas Eve. In just three days, seventy-two hours . . ."

Susan could tell that her sister was already plotting away.

"Let's see," Chris was muttering. "That gives us plenty of time to dig up some more information. Talk to some people—Brian, of course, maybe his boss, Carol. . . . Check out this Mr. Stone a little bit more carefully. . . . See if some of the pieces fit together. . . ."

"Chris! All this is an incredible long shot, isn't it?" Susan protested.

"Well, maybe, but . . ." Chris sighed impatiently. "Look, if it turns out that Mr. Stone *isn't* embezzling hospital funds, if all this really *is* just a rumor, then nothing's been lost, right? Just a little harmless detective work, that's all.

"But just think, Sooz! If it turns out that Mr. Stone *has* been having some shady dealings, and that he *is* responsible for this terrible thing that's about to happen, you and I could actually save the Ridgewood Children's Hospital! We might keep it from having to close down! Wouldn't that be fantastic?"

"Yes, of course it would," Susan admitted. She still sounded a bit reluctant. Even so, Chris could tell that her twin was already starting to come around to her way of thinking.

"As a matter of fact," Chris went on, suddenly sounding a bit mischievous, "I just thought of a code name for our undercover investigation of Mr. Stone and the workings of the Ridgewood Children's Hospital. Something that's right in line with Christmas . . ."

Susan couldn't resist. "All right. What's the code name you thought up?" she asked with a grin.

"The Candy Cane Caper! It's perfect, don't you think?"

"It *is* kind of catchy," Susan had to agree. She thought for a minute, then said, "Well, Chris, you can certainly be persuasive. It's true that, at this point, we don't have very much to go on. Nothing more than a rumor, really. But if there's even the slightest chance that you and I could find out what's going on and keep the children's hospital from having to close. . . . Well, how could I possibly say no to that?"

"Oh, Sooz, I *knew* you'd agree!" She gave her sister a big hug. "Tell me, what was it that convinced you that this was a case for the Pratt twins' unparalleled sleuthing abilities? My clear-cut arguments? My unwillingness to back down? My limitless spirit?"

Susan laughed. "To tell you the truth, Chris, I think it was the code name you came up with. I mean, how could anyone *possibly* resist being part of something called the Candy Cane Caper?"

Nine

Despite the girls' intention of getting the Candy Cane Caper under way immediately, it wasn't until the following day that they were able to do any actual sleuthing on the case. That evening after dinner Emily asked the girls to help her sort out all the things for the bazaar that she'd picked up that day.

Going through each of the handmade items one at a time was a real treat for the twins. And between exclaiming over each one, talking about what techniques must have gone into making it, and then coming up with a price, it took up almost the whole evening. The rest of it was filled with examining all the secondhand items that Emily had acquired from her friends, teapots and pocketbooks and picture frames, and deciding the best way to display them and how much to charge.

By the end of the evening, the twins were exhausted—but certain that the bazaar was going to be a real success.

"One thing's for sure," Susan said with a sigh as she headed up the stairs to her bedroom, her sister in tow, just before midnight. "If we manage to sell half those items at the bazaar on Thursday, we'll be in good shape."

Even though it was the bazaar she was talking about, she was really thinking about the children's Christmas party. She had come up with a brainstorm that evening, an idea that would make the evening more special—and decided to keep it a total secret, even from her twin.

"Just think of the great Christmas Eve celebration we're going to be able to have for the kids!" Chris agreed, her enthusiasm tempered by her fatigue after a long busy day.

She, too, was thinking about something she'd come up with that evening without her sister knowing. She had also decided to carry out her plan totally on her own.

For the moment, both girls, tired from the long evening of making plans and gettig things ready, were absorbed in thinking about the bazaar and the party. By the next morning, however, the Candy Cane Caper was very much on their minds once agian.

The very first thing, over a breakfast of golden-brown waffles with Vermont maple syrup, Susan said to her twin, "So, Chris, are you free for lunch today?"

"Lunch!" Chris cried. "I haven't even finished *breakfast* yet! And at the rate I've been gobbling up these waffles, I doubt that I'll even have *room* for lunch!"

"Trust me, you will," Susan returned with a chuckle. "Anyway, I was thinking . . . Why don't you and I invite Brian out to lunch today so we can talk about . . . well, *you* know. What we talked about last night."

"Sure. I think starting out by talking to an insider is a great idea. But why don't we just meet him over at the hospital cafeteria, the way you did yesterday?"

"Christine Pratt! What kind of sleuth *are* you? We don't want anyone to overhear us talking, naturally! Besides, maybe we should keep out of Mr. Stone's way just so he doesn't see us hanging around the hospital too much."

"Or hanging around with Brian too much either," Chris added. "After all, tackling this case is something that you and I decided to do. We don't want Brian to be implicated, not in any way. After all, if word ever got back to Mr. Stone, he could lose his job."

"You're absolutely right, Chris."

Chris leaned back in her chair, placed her hands on her full stomach, and grinned. "So, Sooz, where shall the three of us have lunch?"

Susan smiled impishly. "Actually, I'd like to take him out to Ridgewood's finest eating establishment, whatever that happens to be."

"Ridgewood's finest eating establishment?" echoed John Pratt, coming into the room. "Hmmm, now let me see. . . ."

"Grandpa!" Chris squealed. "Were you listening in on our conversation again?"

"Eavesdropping, you mean. As a matter of fact, I guess I was." He winked at Susan, then said, "After all, Chris, I'm learning that you're always up to something interesting. Frankly, it would take a lot of willpower to stop listening in on the details of your action-packed life!"

Chris laughed. "*My* life? Action-packed? Hardly!"

"Grandpa," Susan said, "what *is* the best restaurant here in Ridgewood?"

John thought for a few seconds. "Well, there *is* one exceptional restaurant in town. Alfredo's has the best Italian food I've ever had in my life—and that includes that trip to Rome that your grandmother and I took a few years back!"

"Then Alfredo's it is!" Susan exclaimed. "I'll go invite Brian right away. He should be at work by now." She headed for the doorway, then paused. "By the way, Grandpa, does Alfredo's have candles on the table?"

"Why, I believe so."

"And linen tablecloths?"

"Of course!"

"And a bouquet of flowers on every table?"

John Pratt's eyes narrowed suspiciously. "Sounds to me as if you're planning a romantic little lunch."

"Not exactly," Susan returned merrily. "Although I must admit that I wouldn't mind *too* much if there was just a *touch* of romance in the air!"

Chris and Susan arrived at Alfredo's right on time, so they were surprised to find that Brian was already there, gorging himself on garlic bread as he waited for them. The restaurant was everything the girls' grandfather had promised. It was quiet and elegant and even romantic, with all the trimmings that Susan had been hoping for. There were even festive strings of tiny white lights intertwined with pine garlands along the windows.

Most important, it offered them the privacy they would need for their discussion of the hospital's current problems. And what—or *who*—might be responsible for them.

"This is quite a change from yesterday's lunch, Susan, isn't it?" Brian asked with a grin as the girls sat down. "Believe it or not, I've never been here before. But if their garlic bread is any indication of the quality of the rest of their food, I just might start eating here every day!"

But even as the twins were laughing, he grew serious.

"Although if the hospital really does close down soon, that means I'll be out of a job, along with a lot of other people. If that happens, I won't be able to afford lunch at *any* restaurant. Not with the high cost of going to college . . ."

"Brian, that's precisely what we wanted to talk to you about today," Susan interjected.

"And here I thought you girls invited me out to lunch solely because of my charming personality!"

Susan blushed, then said, "Well, that might have had a *little* to do with it. . . . But Chris and I did want to find out more about that rumor you mentioned yesterday. You know, the one about the possibility of Mr. Stone . . . well, having something to do with the hospital's financial troubles."

Puzzled, Brian looked at Susan, then at Chris. "But that has nothing to with either of you! Why on earth would you want to go out of your way to concern yourselves with something like this . . . especially during your vacation?"

Chris grinned at his reaction of surprise. "Let's just say that we Pratt twins have a long history of taking on any project that looks as if it might be the least bit adventurous."

"And we've got a lot of experience in the sleuthing business," Susan went on. "We once spent the night in a haunted house to find out if it really was haunted. Then there was last summer, when we had jobs as camp counselors and we helped keep the camp from having to close down by investigating some mysterious goings-on there. Why, you might say that sticking our noses into other people's business has become sort of a hobby!"

More seriously, she added, "But only if those people need help—and Chris and I agree that we might be able to give it to them."

"Well, the Ridgewood Children's Hospital sure could use some help," Brian said ruefully. "And if you two are willing to give us some, I, for one, would be pretty grateful."

"Good," said Chris. "Then it's settled. Sooz and I are now declaring that the Candy Cane Caper has officially begun."

"The *what*?"

The twins burst out laughing, then went on to explain their habit of nicknaming each one of their adventures. They managed to convince Brian that it made the whole thing that much more fun.

"So where do we begin?" he asked a few minutes later, after they had told the waiter which of the many delicious-sounding pasta dishes listed on the menu each of them wanted to order.

"Tell us more about this rumor," Chris said excitedly.

"Gee, there's not much to tell," said Brian with a shrug. "Just what I told Susan already. And that was something that my boss, Carol, told me. I don't know who told her."

Chris frowned pensively. "Okay. Let me ask you something then. Does Mr. Stone spend a lot of money—more than he probably makes from his job of hospital director, I mean?"

"Gee, that's tough. . . . He's got a nice house, and a new car . . . but aside from that, I really don't know."

Chris frowned, hating to admit that she didn't really know where to go from there. As the waiter placed their lunches on the table, in fact, he glanced over at her with concern.

"Darn!" she complained once the waiter had left. "We're not getting anywhere! How am I supposed to find out if this Mr. Stone is a shifty character or not? I don't even know what he *looks* like!"

"You're about to find out," Susan said calmly, glancing toward the front door of the restaurant. "He just came in."

Chris's jaw dropped open. "Mr. Stone? Really? Oooh, I

can't even see the door from here. Where is he? Can you point him out to me once he sits down?"

"We won't have to," said Brian. "He's just spotted us, and he's on his way over to our table at this very minute!"

Chris's heart was pounding. As far as she knew, she could be about to meet a real criminal—someone who was stealing money from the Ridgewood Children's Hospital!

Or, she reminded herself, you might be about to meet a perfectly nice man who has been unjustly accused of something or at least been the butt of some pretty ugly rumors.

"Well, hello again!" Mr. Stone said in a jovial manner as he reached their table. "Hello, Brian. And hello—wait a minute." He looked from Susan to Chris and back at Susan again. "I remember meeting one of you yesterday, but for the life of me, I can't tell which one it was!"

"It was me." Susan laughed. "My sister Chris and I are identical twins."

"I can see that! So there are two of you, are there?"

Brian introduced Chris to Mr. Stone, and then the four of them chatted for a few minutes about the bazaar, now only a day away, and the Christmas Eve party the following night. Mr. Stone made it clear that he was thrilled about the girls pitching in and rallying the whole town of Ridgewood, planning the bazaar, and putting together a holiday celebration for the children. Chris cast a glance in her twin's direction that said that she, too, found it difficult to believe that this friendly man could be capable of doing anything dishonest.

But then he said something that totally changed their minds.

"Well, I'll let you three get on with your lunch," he said cheerfully. "Great food here. By the way, let me know how you like it. We're planning to open Alfredo's restaurants all over New England some time next year."

Susan nearly choked on the forkful of lasagna she'd just put into her mouth. "We?" she sputtered, trying to sound casual.

"Well, Alfredo himself is the driving force behind the venture. I'm just one of the investors. One of the *major* investors, as a matter of fact," he added with a big grin.

"A *major* investor?" Susan repeated.

"Well . . . you know, something like that doesn't really cost as much as most people might think," he said quickly. He seemed annoyed by her question.

By now Susan was too dumbfounded to speak. Fortunately, her twin was not.

"How many restaurants are you planning to open?" Chris asked sweetly.

Mr. Stone eyed her warily. "Eight of them. You girls sure ask a lot of questions!"

"Well, we'll be sure to let you know how we like the food here," Chris said, wearing a big innocent smile and ignoring his last comment. "I'm sure it'll be just great!"

As soon as Mr. Stone was out of earshot, she turned to her two luncheon companions, her eyes shining and her cheeks flushed pink with excitement.

"Did you hear that?" she squealed. "Did you hear what he just *said*? Mr. Stone is a major investor in a brand-new chain of restaurants. Eight of them!"

"Calm down, Chris," said Susan. "You may be jumping to conclusions."

"Sooz, eight restaurants! We're talking about a lot of money here! Especially if they're all going to be this fancy. All that cash has to come from somewhere!"

"Chris is right," said Brian. "It does sound as if Mr. Stone has suddenly got a lot of money to play around with."

He put down his fork. "All of a sudden I'm not very hungry."

"Don't worry," Chris said reassuringly. "Now that we've got a bit more to go on than just a rumor, I'm more committed than ever to getting to the bottom of the hospital's financial problems. Or at least to finding out if Mr. Stone is the cause of them!"

Enthusiastically she dug into the huge plate of spaghetti in front of her. "Eat up, fellow crime fighters. We've got a big job ahead of us. And we're going to need all the energy we can muster up to get the Candy Cane Caper into high gear!"

Ten

While both Chris and Susan were anxious for the Candy Cane Caper to get under way, they had, at least for the moment, more pressing things to worry about. Planning a bazaar was a big job, and they needed the rest of Wednesday, all afternoon and all evening, to get things ready. It seemed as if there were a million different things to do, yet with each passing moment, with every additional thing they did to get ready, the twins grew more and more excited.

And the fact that their grandparents were both getting so involved made them even happier. Emily Pratt barely had a chance to sit down and have a cup of tea, what with all the running around she was doing, collecting and organizing and telephoning and finishing up some of her own half-completed crafts projects. John Pratt was also caught up in a whirlwind of activity, packing and unpacking all the things that, little by little, were being transported to the community room over at the church.

Finally the big day arrived. Thursday morning was a cold but sunny day without a single snow cloud in the sky—the perfect weather for going to a bazaar, Susan concluded as she hopped out of bed and dashed to the window.

Still in her nightgown, she crept across the hall to her sister's room.

"Chris? Chris?" she whispered, opening the door slowly. "I know it's pretty early, but we've got a lot to do, so I think you'd better get up. . . ."

Once she opened the door, however, she found her twin already dressed, standing in front of the mirror above the dresser brushing her hair.

"Why, *there* you are, Sooz! I thought you'd never wake up! Have you forgotten what today is?"

And then when she saw the look of astonishment on Susan's face, she burst out laughing.

"Come on, Sooz. Let's get down to breakfast. You and I have got a bazaar to run!"

A few hectic hours later, the First Annual Town of Ridgewood Christmas Bazaar was in full swing. The community room was filled with people—and every one of them seemed to be having a good time. There were several dozen folding tables covered in bright red and green tablecloths on which were displayed all the items that were for sale: crafts; cookies, cakes, and pies; secondhand goods; and the things that the local shopkeepers had donated. In the back corner was the display of John Pratt's Christmas trees, scenting the air with the distinct fragrance of pine. Mrs. King was playing Christmas carols on the piano, adding the finishing touch to the holiday atmosphere.

And right in front, between the entrance to the community room and the towering Christmas tree that graced it, was the magnificent gingerbread creation that Susan and her grandmother had made: a house standing almost two feet tall with a gumdrop roof, mint-square windows, and a front door made out of a chocolate bar. White icing dripped over the roof made it look as if it had just snowed. And instead of flowers or bushes, there was a row of candy canes all around the base of the house. It was truly a sight to see, and so far hardly anyone had been able to resist buying a chance to win the totally edible house.

"Wow, this is quite a turnout!" Andy commented, coming over to the table displaying hand-knit items, a varied collection of sweaters and afghans and mittens and mufflers, where the twins were standing. They had just stopped off to say hello to the salesperson—who happened to be Emily Pratt.

"I'll say!" Chris agreed. "I had no idea that this many people lived in Ridgewood!"

"Well, they're not *all* from Ridgewood, you know." Andy cast an odd smile at Chris, in response to her quizzical smile. "Oh, didn't I mention that I put up Susan's posters in some of the neighboring towns?"

"As a matter of fact, you didn't." Chris laughed. "But what a great idea! And I appreciate your going out of your way to help the bazaar be a success. But if you'll excuse me, I'd better go tell Mrs. Washington to start making another batch of her hot apple cider. A very *large* batch!"

"I'll go tell her," Susan offered. "I was just heading over that way, anyway. I see that Brian just came in, and I wanted to go say hello to him."

As she edged through the crowd, however, intent on getting over to the opposite corner of the room, Susan suddenly felt someone grab her arm roughly.

"I want to tell you something," a voice hissed in her ear. "You and your sister are a bunch of busybodies. If you girls know what's good for you, you'll both start minding your own business!"

With a gasp of astonishment, Susan whirled around

. . . and saw Mr. Stone hurrying away from her, trying to disappear into the crowd.

She was still shaken when she reached Brian a few seconds later.

"Hi, Susan!" he greeted her—but his grin quickly turned into a concerned frown. "Hey, what's wrong?"

She pulled him aside, into the corner.

"Brian, the strangest thing just happened! Mr. Stone grabbed me and . . . and *threatened* me!"

"He threatened you? What do you mean?"

Susan told him what had just happened. When she had finished, Brian shook his head slowly and said, "Wow. That sounds pretty serious, doesn't it? You know, I'm one of the last people to believe a rumor, especially a really negative one. But between what happened yesterday at Alfredo's and what just happened here, I'm really beginning to get suspicious!"

Susan nodded. "It does sound as if Mr. Stone is up to something, doesn't it?"

"And as if he wants to make sure that nobody finds out about it!" Earnestly, he said, "I think you'd better back off now, before this whole thing gets messy. It's obvious that Mr. Stone knows you girls suspect something, and who knows how dangerous he might turn out to be? After all, embezzling hospital money is a very serious crime!"

"I know it is." Susan thought for a few seconds, then said, "But don't you see, Brian? That's why it's so important that he *not* get away with it!"

"Wait a minute, Susan. Are you saying that even though Mr. Stone has warned you to keep out of this, you *still* plan to continue with the Candy Cane Caper?"

She sighed. "I can't back down now. Not when every day that I'm here in Ridgewood, I become more and more convinced that Mr. Stone is responsible for the children's hospital's financial problems!"

"But, Susan . . ."

"You don't want Mr. Stone to get away with anything illegal—not to mention totally unethical and just downright *low*—do you?"

"No, but . . ."

"And you don't want the hospital to be forced to close, do you?"

"Of course not!"

"Well, then," Susan said with a resolute nod of her head, "it's settled. Chris and I will continue to try to get to the bottom of this. With your help, of course. You *are* still willing to help us, Brian, aren't you?"

Brian couldn't help laughing. "You're a pretty persuasive person, you know that?"

"Do you think so?" Susan said with a twinkle in her brown eyes. "I guess I must have learned it from one of the experts—my sister!

"Now you and I need to discuss where the Candy Cane Caper should go from here. But all that can wait until later. As for right now, I think I'll have some fun at this bazaar. Do some Christmas shopping over at the craft tables, browse through the books . . . and maybe even buy a chance on that fantastic gingerbread house over there. After all," she added teasingly, "I'm one of the few people in the room who actually knows how good it tastes!"

Susan took Brian by the arm and led him out of the corner in which they'd been chatting, back toward the festivities. "We still have plenty of time for our detective work. As for right now, let's get this Christmas holiday under way!"

Eleven

"Well, girls, I'd say that a hearty round of congratulations is in order," boomed John Pratt as the twins, still half asleep, wandered into their grandmother's dining room in search of some breakfast early Friday morning. "That bazaar of yours really set this town on its ear!"

"That's right," his wife agreed heartily. "And we're not the only ones who think so either!"

"What do you mean?" asked Chris, rubbing her eyes and wondering what on earth everyone was so excited about.

"Just take a look at this morning's headlines, and you'll see exactly what your grandmother means!"

Proudly John Pratt held up the *Ridgewood Express,* the town's weekly newspaper. Sure enough, the headline on the front page read, "Holiday Bazaar a Great Success!" Underneath, in slightly smaller letters, it said, "Visiting Twins Organize Fund-Raising—and Fun-Raising—Event."

"Those visiting twins are you and me," squealed Susan, now fully awake. "Why, we're practically *famous* in this town now!"

"Especially since our faces are plastered all over that front page as well!"

"Where? What are you talking about?" Excitedly Susan grabbed the newspaper away from Chris. And when she looked at the front page more closely, she discovered that indeed, a large photograph of the Pratt twins was right below the headlines, where everyone in the town of Ridgewood was sure to see it.

It was an informal shot, one that the girls hadn't even realized was being taken. Susan and Chris had been photographed while standing in front of the gingerbread house, laughing together and looking pleased that the bazaar that they had organized had turned out to be—just as the headline said—a great success.

"There's a long article about the bazaar, too," John told them. He was obviously just as happy as they were about their sudden, and totally unexpected, stardom. "It's all about how you girls came up with the idea in the first place because you wanted a way to raise money for the kids at the Ridgewood Children's Hospital and all the work you both put into making it happen.

"As a matter of fact," he went on with a wink, "even Emily and I are mentioned in the article . . . for all the work *we* put in!"

"That's wonderful!" Susan frowned pensively. "But there's one thing I don't understand. How did the reporter for the *Express* know so much about what went on behind the scenes? I mean, no one asked me anything about it. . . ."

"That's exactly what I was going to ask," her twin added. "We had no inkling that there was going to be an article. Yet someone managed to find out every little detail. . . ."

"That's easy!" Just then Andy strode into the dining

room, grinning broadly. "The reporter who wrote that article—who happens to be Betty's niece, I might add—got all her information from—shall we say an inside source?"

"You're just full of surprises, Andy Connors, aren't you?" Chris chuckled. "First you put up posters all over the entire area, helping make our bazaar as big a success as it was. And then you tell this reporter from the *Express*, Betty's niece, all about us. . . ."

"And turn you both into local celebrities." Teasingly, Andy finished that sentence. "You deserve it, too. You both did a great job—and for a very good cause, too, I might add."

"That reminds me," Chris said, suddenly serious. "All this praise may be well and good, but Sooz and I still have some more work to do. Some very important work. We have to get going to the children's Christmas Eve celebration. Tonight is Christmas Eve, don't forget!"

"Work, work, work," Andy teased. "Don't you girls ever have any fun?"

Susan and Chris looked at each other and smiled.

"Andy," said Susan, "the work that we do *is* fun!"

As soon as they had finished breakfast, the twins got busy getting things ready for that evening's Christmas party. Fortunately, the bazaar had raised enough money for them to buy decorations, refreshments, and presents for all the children. In addition, they had the contributions of toys and books that some of the local shopkeepers had made . . . and a wonderful bonus that they hadn't been counting on.

As they were about to leave the house late that morning to go over to the hospital and start setting things up, the girls received a telephone call.

"Hello," said a strange voice. "I'd like to speak to one

of the twins who organized the Christmas bazaar yesterday, please."

"This is Christine Pratt speaking." She couldn't help wondering who on earth was calling her . . . and why.

"My name is Frank Pierce. . . ."

"That name sounds awfully familiar," Chris commented.

"I was mentioned in the newspaper article this morning. I'm the person who won the gingerbread house in the drawing yesterday."

"Oh, yes." By now Chris was more puzzled than ever.

"Well, uh, I bought a chance on that house to help the hospital raise money. And I was astonished when I won, since I never really expected to. But to tell the truth, I'm a bachelor who lives all alone, and now that I've got this fantastic cookie house sitting on my kitchen table, I realize that I don't really have any use for it."

There was a long pause, and then he said, "So if it's okay with you, I'd like to donate it to the Ridgewood Children's Hospital. I have a feeling that the kids over there could get a lot more use out of it than I ever could! Do . . . do you think that's a good idea?"

"Do I!" Chris cried. "Just tell me your address, Mr. Pierce, and I'll be right over to pick it up!"

Although the girls were busy getting everything ready for the children's party, they didn't forget about the Candy Cane Caper. As a matter of fact, Chris kept insisting that Christmas Eve was the best time to carry out their undercover work.

"After all," she told Susan as the girls headed down to the basement in search of Brian as soon as they reached the hospital, "things are bound to be a little disorganized today. I'm sure that many of the people who work here are planning their own little parties, so they won't notice if we do a little snooping around the place. Besides, the main person we have to worry about is Mr. Stone, and chances are he's taken today off!''

Susan nodded in agreement. "Okay, Chris. You're right. But where do we start?"

"That's easy. Mr. Stone's office, of course."

"Christine Pratt! We can't go into his office! Why, that's . . . that's private property!"

"So are the hospital's funds," Chris retorted. "Come on, Susan. I know that taking a look around Mr. Stone's office is prying. But how else are we going to find out whether or not he's involved in dishonest dealings?"

Susan frowned. "Well, you've got a point. . . . Besides, maybe it's not even locked. Maybe it wouldn't hurt if we just stuck our heads in and took a peek. . . ."

"Well, there's only one way to find out!" By that time, the girls were right outside Mr. Stone's office. There was no light shining underneath the door, so it was a pretty safe bet that no one was in there. Chris looked up and down the corridor, saw that no one else was around, and put her hand on the doorknob.

It didn't move.

She was about to inform her sister that Mr. Stone's office was locked. Chris jumped.

"And what do you girls think you're doing?" boomed an angry male voice, seemingly from out of nowhere.

Even before the twins spun around, their faces flushed pink, they knew who that voice belonged to—and that Mr. Stone had just caught them, red-handed, trying to break into his office.

"We . . . uh . . . I . . ." Chris sputtered, still clutching the doorknob.

Her sister, however, did some fast thinking.

"Why, hello, Mr. Stone," she said, her voice only shaking a bit. "We were just trying to get into Brian

Barker's office. He told us we could store the children's Christmas presents in here. . . ."

"What do you mean, Brian Barker's office?" Mr. Stone demanded. "This isn't Brian's office!"

"It's not?" Susan summoned up all her acting abilities— and managed to do a pretty convincing imitation of someone who was sincerely baffled. "But I thought . . . he said . . ."

"Brian's office is across the hall." He sneered. "Can't you girls read?"

Wearing an expression of total innocence, Susan glanced up and pretended to read the sign on the door for the very first time.

"Why, you're right!" she cried, sounding truly amazed. "This isn't Brian's office at all. This is *your* office, Mr. Stone!"

"And I'll thank you two to keep away from it."

"Oh, of course! Of course! Well, see you at tonight's Christmas party," Susan said brightly. And she started to move across the hall, toward the door to the computer room—Brian's *real* office.

But all of a sudden Mr. Stone lunged toward her and grabbed her arm roughly, the same way he had the day before, at the bazaar.

"You're darn right you'll be seeing me at the Christmas party tonight! And I expect to see you, too. *Both* of you. If I catch either one of you sneaking off during the party, trespassing in this hospital, poking your noses into places where they don't belong . . . Well, just don't say I didn't warn you girls!"

With that, he opened the door to his office with a key, returned the key to his pocket, and disappeared inside, slamming the door behind him.

Chris and Susan immediately retreated into the computer room.

"Gee, Sooz," Chris finally said. "He sure sounded mean!"

"And he sounded as if he meant what he said, too!"

"*Now* what are we going to do?"

"Why, what do you mean, Chris?" Susan was genuinely surprised. "You're not going to let a few vague threats discourage us from going ahead with the Candy Cane Caper, are you?"

"Well . . . it *is* becoming more and more apparent that Mr. Stone is guilty. And we can't do a thing about it until we find some proof."

"Right. And that proof is obviously in his office somewhere. Otherwise he wouldn't be so upset that we were prowling around outside it."

"But you heard what he said, Sooz. He's going to be at the Christmas party tonight, and he expects us both to be there. How can we possibly be in two places at once—both at the party *and* down here looking for the evidence we need?"

There was a long pause . . . and then Susan said softly, "Christine Pratt, I can't believe you just asked me that. Have you forgotten that you and I are masters of disguise? Not to mention experts at fooling people . . ."

Chris's jaw dropped open. "Sooz! You're not suggesting that we . . . you're not saying that you and I . . ."

"Of course!" Susan returned matter-of-factly. "Why, what better way of getting around that nasty Mr. Stone than taking advantage of the fact that you and I are identical twins in order to trick him?"

"Well . . . okay," Chris agreed with a sigh. But then she grinned. "Oh, boy. Another chance to switch identities!"

"Or at least borrow each other's for a little while!"

Just then Brian came into the computer room.

"There you are!" he exclaimed. "I've been looking for you. Didn't you say you wanted some help sneaking all those Christmas presents in here?"

"You bet. The trunk of our grandparents' car is bursting with presents, and this would be the perfect place to keep them until tonight," said Chris. "But before we start unloading them, there's something we want to tell you about."

She proceeded to tell him about the little scene they'd just had with Mr. Stone—and their belief that there was something—papers or reports or files—in his office that might incriminate him. She finished by asking him if he had any idea what those papers might be.

Brian's response was to shake his head slowly and look discouraged.

"I'm afraid you're not going to have much luck," he said. "The reason that they hired us computer people in the first place was to eliminate all that paperwork. Practically every piece of information about the hospital—reports, memos, budgets, billing files—is on a computer disk. So even if you could get into Mr. Stone's office, you wouldn't be able to sit there and look through his files. . . ."

Instead of becoming discouraged, however, both Chris's and Susan's brown eyes lit up.

"Computer disks!" Chris cried. "Of course! If that's where the hospital's financial information is stored, then that's the best place to look for something that would tie Mr. Stone into its money problems! Oh, Brian, you've got to help us!"

Brian gulped. "Well, sure, Chris. But . . . but how?"

Chris thought for a few seconds. "You've got to teach one of us how to operate the computer system."

"What?" Brian was flabbergasted.

"Well, you told me yourself that operating the computers here was pretty straightforward," Susan reminded him. "Remember? It was as we were driving to the hospital on Monday. . . ."

"I don't know. . . . Do either of you girls know anything about computers?"

"I do," Chris piped up. "A little, anyway. We have them at our high school, back in Whittington."

"And Chris is a math whiz," Susan added. "If anyone can learn how to work your computers quickly, it's Chris."

"Wait a minute." Brian still wasn't convinced. "Let's say that over the next hour or so, while everybody's at lunch, I teach Chris how to operate our computers. How are you girls going to get ahold of the disks in Mr. Stone's office in the first place?"

"Leave that up to us," Chris said with a confident wave of her hand. "Sooz and I are experts at that sort of thing."

"Okay. Let's say the two of you manage—somehow—to get the disks and use the computer to find out what's on them. What about the party? Mr. Stone is sure to show up, and he expects both of you girls to be there, too."

"That's the easiest part," Susan replied with a mischievous smile. "During the party while Chris is looking for evidence, *I'll* stand in for her at the party. Some of the time, anyway."

Brian frowned. "I'm afraid I still don't follow. . . ."

"It's simple. I'll be Susan—myself—for a while. You know, I'll show up at the party dressed the way I usually dress, introduce myself to all the kids, make sure Mr. Stone sees me. Then I'll slip off to wash my hands—and then Chris will show up. Or at least someone who looks just like Chris, and who dresses the way she does and acts the way she does. . . ."

"Oh, I get it!" Brian shook his head slowly. "You'll be both Chris *and* Susan, one at a time. It sounds like a great idea. A brainstorm, in fact. But isn't that going to be a bit difficult to carry off?"

"Not for us!" Chris laughed. "All we need is two sets of clothes, a little bit of acting ability . . . and a whole lot of bravery!"

"That's right. And we know from experience that when it comes to something like the Candy Cane Caper," Susan went on, wearing a big grin, "we Pratt twins happen to have all three of those key ingredients. *Especially* the third!"

Twelve

Right from the start, it was apparent to everyone that the Christmas Eve celebration was going to be one that the patients at the Ridgewood Children's Hospital would never forget. Ever since the children had first heard about the party, they hadn't been able to think or talk about anything else. Spirits were high as they hurried to the sun-room on the hospital's top floor at seven o'clock that evening. Many of them were dressed in their bathrobes and slippers—and practically all of them were whispering and giggling in gleeful anticipation of the evening ahead.

As soon as they saw the sun-room, the children knew they weren't about to be disappointed. A huge Christmas tree, the largest one that John Pratt and Andy had been able to find, was set up in one corner, decorated with strings of popcorn, candy canes, and tiny white lights that had been donated by Alfredo himself. Underneath the tree were dozens and dozens of packages wrapped up in pretty red and green paper and ribbons, each one with a gift tag bearing the name of one of the children.

In the opposite corner was a table laden with Christmas

cookies, hot apple cider . . . and, in the middle, Susan and Emily Pratt's magnificent gingerbread house. There were other decorations as well, and Christmas carols were playing in the background. The twins themselves were all decked out in their holiday finery: Chris in black wool pants and the distinctive red and green hand-knit sweater that her grandmother had made her for Christmas the year before, Susan in a red velveteen jumper and a white ruffled blouse. Their short chestnut-brown hair was brushed back off their faces in identical styles. They both looked lovely—all dressed up and ready for a party.

Everything was perfect—except for one small thing. The room was very warm, so warm, in fact, that some of the windows were open. Instead of being annoyed that the heat was turned up as high as it was, however, the twins were pleased. After all, they were the ones who had sneaked into the closet where the thermostat was and turned the heat way up high late that afternoon. . . .

Susan and Chris had been busy all day—but as soon as they saw the joyful expressions on the children's faces, their huge smiles and their shining eyes, they knew it had all been worth it.

"Wow! Just *look* at this place!" exclaimed Danny when he saw the sun-room. His eyes grew as round as the holly wreath that was hanging on the door. "I don't even feel like I'm in the hospital anymore!"

Chris and Susan looked at each other and grinned triumphantly. After all, that was exactly what they had been hoping for.

"Hey, am I seeing things?" cried Brian as he came in. "You girls have really done a job on this place!"

"Glad you like it," returned Chris. In a much softer voice, she added, "Now if we can only do *half* as effective a job on our *second* mission for this evening . . . !"

Brian acknowledged her comment with a wink. Then he went on to say, in a loud voice, "But, gee, it sure is hot in here! Do you suppose there's something wrong with the heat?"

"Maybe," Chris replied, just as loudly. "If it doesn't get cooler soon, I'll go track down someone from maintenance and ask him if he can turn it down."

It wasn't long before the sun-room—now the Ridgewood Children's Hospital's official Christmas headquarters—was filled with children, nurses, doctors, and other hospital personnel. And, of course, Mr. Stone himself.

The very first thing he did was survey the room, pick Susan and Chris out of the crowd, and make a beeline in their direction.

"I'm glad to see that you're both here," he said, his tone congenial but the look in his eyes meaningful. "And I'm looking forward to a long evening here at the party."

"That's great, Mr. Stone," Chris said, sounding both hearty and convincing. "The more the merrier, I always say. Of course, both Sooz and I expect to be pretty busy. There's still a lot to do, you know. Running a party for a few dozen kids isn't exactly the easiest thing in the world!"

"Don't worry," Susan interjected. "We'll manage. We'll just have to stay on our toes, that's all!"

The glance that the twins exchanged went unnoticed by Mr. Stone.

"It is awfully hot in here, though," Mr. Stone went on to say, loosening his tie and looking very uncomfortable. "The heat's been turned way up ever since this afternoon. I'd better talk to the maintenance people. . . ."

"That's all right, I'll do it," Chris offered. "As soon as things get under way. In the meantime, all the windows are open—see?"

By that point, all the children had arrived, and it was time for the party. Singing Christmas carols seemed like the best way to get things rolling, and Mrs. King had cheerfully agreed to the twins' suggestion that she repeat her performance of the day before, playing holiday melodies on the piano, this time for the children's benefit.

"Boys and girls, we're lucky enough to have a fine entertainer here with us this evening," Chris announced in her best mistress-of-ceremonies voice. "Eleanor King will be playing some Christmas classics, and we can all sing along. Who knows? This might turn out to be the very first performance of what becomes the Ridgewood Children's Hopital Chorus!"

As Mrs. King began with "Oh, Little Town of Bethlehem," Susan and Chris made a point of standing right next to Mr. Stone.

"It's so hot," Susan complained in a loud whisper. "Why don't you go see what you can do, Chris?"

Chris pretended to be somewhat reluctant. "Well . . . okay. I am enjoying the music, but you're right: It *is* hot." With that, she left the sun-room.

As soon as she left, Chris stopped in at the washroom right across the hall from the sun-room, slipped off her pants and sweater and left them hanging on a hook in one of the stalls, and changed into the jeans and blue and white sweater she had stored there before the party began.

Once that was accomplished and she was hurrying down the hall toward the stairs, Chris became aware of how hard her heart was pounding. This mission was turning out to be scarier than she'd anticipated. She was about to break into Mr. Stone's office, look through his possessions, steal into the computer room, and examine whatever computer disks she managed to find . . . all as quickly and as silently as she could. Not to mention as thoroughly as she could . . .

knowing the whole time that at any moment she could be discovered.

Even so, it was too late to turn back now. Not that she really wanted to. Not when she thought about the possibility that the children's hospital might close . . . and that Mr. Stone could very well be the cause.

Chris dashed down to the main floor and then slipped out the back door. By now her nervousness had vanished. She was too busy carrying out the carefully thought-out steps of the Candy Cane Caper.

She was anxious to see if the brainstorm she'd had earlier that day had worked. Sure enough, as she neared the section of the building where the window in Mr. Stone's office was, she saw right away that her plan had been successful. Since she and Brian had turned up the heat so high, everyone, including Mr. Stone, had been forced to open the windows in their offices. His was open just a bit . . . but all she needed was a space big enough for her to fit her fingers in. After that, pulling it open the rest of the way was a snap. And since his office was in the basement, the tiny window was at ground level, the perfect height for a slim, nimble girl to slip through.

That was exactly what she did after brushing away some of the snow that was piled up next to the building. Getting into Mr. Stone's office was simple, thanks to a bit of forethought. Now she had to find the computer disks, and she had to work quickly. . . .

Susan, meanwhile, waited a few minutes, until Mr. Stone was totally absorbed in singing, "Hark, the Herald Angels Sing!" along with all the children. Then she slipped away, into the washroom across the hall. With lightning speed she took off her jumper and blouse and pulled on Chris's pants and sweater. After a quick peek in the mirror just to make sure that she did, indeed, look just like her twin sister, she dashed back to the sun-room once again.

At that point, Mrs. King took out a carton filled with musical instruments, mostly bells, and she invited each child to take an instrument, gather around the piano, and accompany her as she played and sang, "Jingle Bells." There was quite a bit of commotion as everyone scampered around the room excitedly, and Susan-as-Chris pretended to bump right into Mr. Stone.

"Ooops—sorry," she said, sounding as casual as Chris would have in such a situation. "Guess I'd better try watching where I'm going. Well, I found someone from maintenance, all right. He said the thermostat is stuck or something, so it'll be a while until things get back to normal. But don't worry, he's working on it." She flashed him a big smile, then went over to the piano to join the others.

So far so good, Susan-as-Chris was thinking as she heartily sang, "Dashing through the snow . . ."

Downstairs, her sister had just dropped from the open window onto the floor of Mr. Stone's office. Because all the windows in the hospital were open, she could hear from up above, the children singing, "Jingle Bells." But she was too wrapped up in what she was doing to appreciate the fact that their celebration was already turning out to be a lot of fun for them. Stealthily she opened drawers and cabinets, hoping to stumble upon some computer disks . . . but all she found were office supplies and papers, none of which looked relevant.

Finally, on the edge of despair, Chris stood in the middle of the small office and looked around one more time. There just *had* to be something in here somewhere, yet she had checked every drawer, every file . . . everything. And nothing had turned up. . . .

And then she spotted Mr. Stone's briefcase. It was tucked behind a coat rack, on which his gray wool coat was hung. It was a long shot, she knew, but she was running out of alternatives. Carefully, nervously, she placed the leather briefcase on the desk and undid the two gold locks.

Please, please, let them be in here, she was thinking as she opened it up.

Upstairs, Susan noticed that Mr. Stone was looking around the room nervously . . . and she was afraid he might be noticing that Chris's twin sister was nowhere to be found.

"Excuse me, Mr. Stone," she asked him with a big smile. "Is there a bathroom on this floor?"

"Right across the hall," he replied, still looking around the room.

"Great," she said, and she bounded out of the room.

No more than three minutes later, when Mr. Stone saw Susan in the room once again, he looked noticeably relieved.

As Mr. Stone and Susan were discussing the possibility of another snowfall, Chris was five floors below, peering inside Mr. Stone's briefcase.

They're here! she was thinking, tempted to yelp with glee but remembering just in time that this wasn't the time and place to be making any noise, even with the children's chorus covering up whatever sounds she couldn't help making.

Indeed, there were several computer disks inside the briefcase, along with a few other things that obviously belonged to Mr. Stone. There were labels stuck on the upper left-hand corner of each one, and Chris glanced through them. Most of them were Patient Billing or Memos or other categories that were of little interest to her.

But two of them looked *very* interesting. One was

labeled, Budget Submitted. And the other was labeled Budget Revised.

Two budgets, Chris thought with an earnest frown. Now that's interesting. Why on earth would a hospital have *two* budgets?

There was only one way to find out.

As she left Mr. Stone's office, she closed the door gently behind her, but not until she had placed a small piece of cardboard against the bolt so that while the office appeared to be closed up, exactly the way that Mr. Stone had left it, the door wouldn't really be locked.

The computer room was deserted, just as she had known it would be. Chris hurried over to the computer terminal that Brian always used and, mumbling the directions he had given her only that day, turned the machine on, slipped in the disks, and booted up.

I hope I can remember everything, she thought nervously. She punched in the password, followed the instructions she had worked so hard to memorize . . . sure enough, as she pushed the keys and typed in the proper responses, a list of figures entitled "Budget Submitted" appeared on the screen.

Quickly she jotted down some of the figures. "Grounds Upkeep," for example, was listed as costing $10,000. She was tempted to copy the whole thing onto paper, but she was in too much of a hurry to see what the other disk, the Budget Revised, was all about.

As soon as she pressed the right keys and brought the information stored on the second disk onto the screen, Chris's mouth dropped open. The format of this budget was the same . . . but the additional numbers on it astonished her. Next to "Grounds Upkeep," it said, "Budgeted: $10,000." Then it said, "Actual cost: $8,000. Difference: $2,000."

So *that* was what Mr. Stone was doing! He had submitted a budget that indicated that hospital costs were higher than they actually were, then kept the difference for himself! He *was* embezzling money from the hospital . . . and in Chris's hands was tangible proof.

We've done it! she thought, turning off the computer, then rushing back to Mr. Stone's office and putting everything back in order once again before locking it up and heading toward the stairs, with the computer disks tucked safely into her purse. The Candy Cane Caper worked! I managed to find proof that Mr. Stone is, indeed, stealing from the hospital! All I have to do is show it to the board, and he'll be fired . . . and brought up for criminal charges. Then the Ridgewood Children's Hospital can hire a new director—an *honest* director—and it won't have to close after all!

As she hurried toward the sun-room, so thrilled over what she had just discovered that she felt as if she were ready to burst, Chris could hear the children laughing and clapping. Telling Susan and Brian about what she had found would have to wait a while. After all, it sounded as if the surprise she had been planning ever since Thursday, having Andy Connors put in a surprise appearance at the party dressed as Santa Claus himself, had finally come off—and she couldn't wait to see the look on everyone's face. *Especially* her twin's!

But as she strode into the sun-room, *Chris's* expression was the one that caused everyone to break into merry laughter. She was amazed to see that there were *two* Santa Clauses in the room, handing out the presents to the children.

"What . . . ? How . . . ?"

Her sister immediately came to her aid.

"Christine Pratt," she accused in a teasing voice, "are

you the person responsible for recruiting our second Santa?"

"A second Santa?" Chris was still too surprised to be able to figure out what was going on. "All I did was ask Andy to dress up as Santa Claus and show up at the party tonight. It was supposed to be a surprise for everyone—including you!"

"Oh, I was surprised, all right!" Susan replied with a chuckle. "Especially since *I* had arranged for *Grandpa* to come to our celebration dressed as Santa!"

Just then Danny came over to the girls with a few of his friends in tow.

"Susan," he asked shyly, "this is a really nice Christmas party that you girls put together for us kids and all, and we really do appreciate it . . . but how come there are *two* Santa Clauses here?"

Susan and Chris just looked at each other, totally at a loss for an explanation.

Fortunately, Brian happened to overhear Danny, and he rushed to the girls' aid.

"You mean you didn't know, Danny?" he said with surprise. "There are not one but *two* Santas living in the North Pole and bringing presents to children all around the world. You see, Santa Claus has a twin—just like Chris and Susan here. Otherwise, he could never accomplish all the things he does at Christmastime. Why, how could anybody expect just one person to make all those toys and deliver them, not to mention managing the elves and taking care of the reindeer. . . ."

"Really?" Danny asked, not sure if he believed Brian but wanting to very badly. "You mean there really is a Santa Claus—and he's *twins*? Wow!" And he rushed off to tell the rest of his friends.

"So we've got two Santas instead of just one," Brian said with a chuckle.

The look on his face, however, told Chris that he was much more interested in hearing about whether or not the Candy Cane Caper had succeeded than discussing Santa Claus's longtime secret.

"Well, well, well, this is certainly a night of double trouble," Chris said with a huge smile. "Two twins, two Santas . . . and two computer disks, one with the budget that Mr. Stone submitted to the board, and one that showed what expenses *really* were—and how much he was able to keep for himself."

"You're kidding!" Susan squealed. "You mean you actually managed to find proof that Mr. Stone . . . ."

"Careful, here he comes," Brian warned.

"Mr. Stone!" Chris cried boldly. "Are you having a nice time at our party?"

He looked puzzled. "Why, Chris, I just *told* you that I was. . . ." All of a sudden his expression changed as he realized what had been going on—and that he had been fooled.

"Why, you . . . Where were you for the last hour?" he demanded.

"I've been right here, of course," Chris answered, looking innocent. "But I'm afraid I'm going to have to leave now. Susan, can you and the two Santas handle things here for the rest of the evening?"

Susan, wearing a knowing smile, nodded.

"Good. Then, Brian, would you do me a favor?"

"Sure, Chris. Anything."

"Great. How about driving me over to the house of the president of the hospital board right now? I have a little tidbit of information that I'd like to share. . . ."

"You're on!" Brian grinned. "After all, aren't we all trying our best to make this Christmas as merry as possible for everyone here at the Ridgewood Children's Hospital?"

Mr. Stone's eyes narrowed suspiciously. "What are you kids talking about?"

"Oh, nothing," Chris replied loftily. "Or should I say, you'll find out soon enough, Mr. Stone."

As she and Brian headed for the door, one of the nurses came rushing over to her.

"Chris, all of us here at the hospital really appreciate what you've done for the kids—and the rest of us, too. What a wonderful Christmas present!"

"This is nothing," Chris called over her shoulder as she and Brian strode out together. "Just wait until you find out about the *real* Christmas present we've got in store for all of you!"

Thirteen

"Right now," said Susan with a long, contented sigh, *"I* feel as if I'm sitting in the middle of a Christmas card!"

"I know exactly what you mean," her twin agreed amiably. "A Christmas card just like the very first one we received this holiday season, the one with the snow scene on it. Only *this* card shows what's going on *inside* all those snow-covered houses!"

It was late Christmas Eve, just before midnight, and Chris and Susan were lounging in front of the fireplace in their grandparents' living room, sipping hot chocolate. Four stockings had been hung on the mantel earlier that evening, and they were already filled to bursting—with a big, colorful candy cane peeking out of each one. Underneath the tree were stacks of gaily wrapped presents, their bright ribbons reflecting the red and green and gold lights strung throughout the branches. Outside, fat white snowflakes were falling gently, completing the perfect Christmas scene.

But even more important than all the outward signs of Christmas was the way the twins were feeling. What a busy week it had been! First the bazaar, then the Christmas party for the children over at the hospital, finally the Candy Cane Caper.

And they couldn't help being satisfied with all three of

their accomplishments. Now that the president of the Ridgewood Children's Hospital's board of directors knew about the two different budgets that Chris had found in the director's briefcase, there was no doubt that Mr. Stone would be fired and charged with the crime of embezzling. And since the costs of running the hospital would, indeed, be lower now, it wouldn't have to close after all. As Brian had pointed out earlier in the week, that was good news for both the children in that area of Vermont and the adult residents of Ridgewood and all its neighboring towns.

"Well, girls," said Emily Pratt, "it's just too bad that you girls didn't have much of a vacation, with all the running around you did for the bazaar and the party and all. You were so busy all week that you hardly had a chance to enjoy yourselves!"

"Oh, that's all right," Susan replied heartily. "Chris and I had fun planning and organizing . . . and sleuthing, of course. As a matter of fact, we ended up having at *least* as much fun as we would have had if we'd spent the whole week skiing and skating and building snowmen!"

"And tomorrow it's Christmas Day already," Chris observed. "Now that you mention it, I *am* looking forward to a day of rest."

"And having a big dinner, with Danny coming over to be our special guest . . ."

"And opening our presents, too!" Chris added teasingly, gesturing toward the enticing pile of gifts already sitting underneath the Christmas tree. "Don't forget about *that* part of the holiday!"

She grew serious then. "Gee, this week *did* go by quickly, didn't it? Just think, Monday morning we'll have to go back to Whittington. Of course, it'll be great to see Mom and Dad again when they come home from Mexico on Monday night. . . ."

Just then, as the old grandfather clock in the hall struck

twelve times, there was a knock at the door. All four automatically looked at the front door—and then at each other.

"Who could *that* be?" asked Chris.

"I can't imagine," replied her twin. "After all, it *is* Christmas Eve. And it's so late!"

"Maybe it's Santa Claus." John Pratt had a twinkle in his eyes. "The *real* Santa Claus, that is."

"You mean *one* of the real Santa Clauses," Chris countered with a chuckle. "Since we all know now that they're really twins . . ."

There was a second knock at the front door, even louder this time.

"Well, whoever it is doesn't deserve to be left standing outside on a cold snowy winter night," said Emily Pratt. "Whoever is knocking on our door is welcome to come sit by our fire and warm up."

A few seconds later, the twins and their grandfather heard her unlock the front door—and they heard a familiar voice say, "Merry Christmas! Tell me, is there any room here for a cold, tired couple desperately in need of a place to stay?"

"Daddy!" Chris and Susan cried in unison, rushing over to the door so quickly that they nearly knocked over their mugs of hot chocolate.

"What are you two *doing* here?" Chris squealed as she reached the front door and saw both her parents standing on the porch, laden with suitcases and packages that were dusted with snow—and wearing sheepish smiles.

"Would you believe that we couldn't bear to be away from all our loved ones on Christmas?" the twins' mother asked with a smile.

"That's right," her husband agreed. "Somehow, sitting around on a beach, looking at palm trees and working on our tans and drinking iced tea, surrounded by complete strangers, made us both feel that we were missing out on Christmas entirely."

"And we didn't realize how much Christmas meant to us until we were on the verge of doing without it."

"So," Mr. Pratt finished with a shrug, "here we are! We sure missed you girls!"

"We missed you, too!" cried Susan, hugging her mother, then her father.

"And we couldn't be happier that you changed your plans," Emily Pratt said warmly. "Now come on in and get warm. You must be freezing—not to mention exhausted!"

"Not anymore," said her son, putting his arm around her shoulders. "Now that I'm here with all of you, there's no way I'm going to go to sleep and miss out on catching up on everything. That is, assuming that my favorite twins managed to find something interesting to do with their vacation from school!"

Chris and Susan and Emily and John all looked at each other and then burst out laughing.

"Oh, you know us, Daddy," Chris said offhandedly. "Sooz and I always manage to find *something* to keep us both busy!"

"Well," their father said hesitantly, "we hope you're not sick of Vermont already. Your mother and I were thinking of staying on here for a few days. Would you mind if we extended your stay here until next week?"

"*Mind!*" the girls cried in unison.

"Good. Then it's settled," said their mother. "We can't wait to tell you all about our vacation in sunny Mexico, but first tell us what's new here."

"Oh, nothing much," John Pratt said.

The twins exchanged glances.

"Aren't you forgetting something, Grandpa?"

"What are you talking about, Christine?"

"Isn't there something you wanted to tell Mom and Dad . . . about the house here in Vermont, I mean?"

The twins' father looked puzzled. "The house? What about the house?"

John and Emily Pratt looked at each other and then started to chuckle.

"Well," John said after clearing his throat, "it all sounds pretty silly now, but believe it or not, up until a few days ago, Emily and I were actually toying with the idea of selling the house and moving to a condominium down south. You know, in one of those retirement villages."

"Selling the house!" the girls' mother cried.

"Moving south!" her husband echoed.

"See," Emily Pratt said sheepishly, "we *told* you it was a silly idea! Actually, it was the twins here who convinced us of how silly it really was. They showed us that we were still energetic and, well, young at heart. As a matter of fact, I'm about to start a second career!"

"Grandma!" Susan gasped. "This is a real surprise!"

"See, you girls aren't the only ones who are full of secrets! Yes, I've decided to start selling some of the things I make at Betty's Craft Supplies store. She's going to be converting part of it into a gift shop, and she and I and some of the other local craftspeople will be displaying some of our work for sale.

"And," she added with a twinkle in her eyes, "if it goes well, I may even approach some of the shopkeepers over at the local mall!"

"Grandma, that's fantastic!" Chris cried.

"I'll say," Susan agreed. "Wow, this has really turned out to be the perfect Christmas. Mom and Dad are here, I've got the best sister in the world, Grandma and Grandpa have decided not to sell the house after all . . ."

Susan looked around the room at her family, her brown eyes glowing. "You know, for the very first time in my life, I think I really am beginning to appreciate the true meaning of Christmas. Merry Christmas, everybody!"

About the Author

Cynthia Blair grew up on Long Island, earned her B.A. from Bryn Mawr College in Pennsylvania, and went on to get a M.S. in marketing from M.I.T. She worked as a marketing manager for food companies but now has abandoned the corporate life in order to write.

She lives on Long Island with her husband, Richard Smith, and their son Jesse.